DO NOT DISTURB

A PSYCHOLOGICAL THRILLER

NADIJA MUJAGIC

To all trauma survivors—
love yourselves

PART 1

PROLOGUE

FELECIA MEBANE - ONE YEAR EARLIER—JUNE 20,
7:47 P.M.

No one believes *some* people are capable of murder. And then they see it. With their own eyes. And it's very shocking.

For me, today is *that* day.

I pull into the parking lot and eye the spot closest to the building. It's raining with a vengeance. The state of Nevada doesn't see this type of calamity very often. It's like God was making a perfect day to kill someone. When no one is out and about. When no one is watching.

Except for me, of course.

Roger and I are supposed to grab dinner after work; his car was in a repair shop across town. It seems an unusual occurrence, since his car, an Audi, is nearly brand new. He says something about his brakes not working properly; I don't remember. Not important.

He sent me a quick text when the clouds rolled in and asked me to pick him up. Usually, he'd walk home earlier, but he had urgent things to take care of, plus, I highly doubt he even owns an umbrella.

I gaze at the dashboard and see it's almost eight. I'm ten minutes early. Just waiting. Looking out the window. Trying my best.

The windshield is a sheet of rain. The wipers move from side to side at mad speed. I don't think I've ever seen so much rain in one place. My eyes rest on the building. No one could tell there was once a flourishing business between those walls when you look at it—old paint, chipping façade—and especially not in the shitty weather like this.

From my vantage point and distance, the entire building looks like a dollhouse. I can see the first and the second floor, and the stairs in between. The windows are large enough, and because it's already dark outside and the lights are on, I can see all the action inside.

The commotion inside on the second floor stops me in my tracks. I lean forward and strain my eyes to see better between the movement of the wipers.

I never expected to see this, the scene unfolding in front of me. Of all places, it's in Roger's office building.

Bold choice, if you ask me.

Roger isn't even aware of what he looks like when his body gets twisted with rage. It's like his face no longer belongs to him. It always happens when he's scared.

He seems to be yelling at his partner, William—a man in his early sixties, already dreaming of retirement.

They've worked together since they founded the business, though they've never fully seen eye to eye. William has always been the brains behind the operation, while Roger played the charmer, closing deals and keeping clients happy.

It worked for a long time—until it didn't. Success bred resentment, each of them convinced he was the real reason the company thrived. Inflated egos. They are killers.

Perhaps they could be kept in check, but when everything started to fall apart, they turned that resentment on each other, pointing fingers as the business slid off a cliff.

William's staring at Roger from his wheelchair; his poker face is frozen; his eyes are boring on Roger. I know William well enough that, when shit hits the fan, he dunks and makes it. He's not easily rattled. When you look at him, you can never tell what he's thinking about.

I lean even closer and curse the rain under my breath. But I can see most of it, though: Roger flailing his arms, pointing his finger at William, his mouth moving rapidly...

I wonder what Roger is screaming about, but I can only guess it's about their failing business. Roger must be putting all the blame on William.

My eyes are glued to the windshield. Should I record the carnage on my phone? I can use it as evidence later on if it comes to that. Blackmail. I reach for it, but it's somewhere else... I can't locate it.

"Shit!" things always disappear whenever I need them.

I turn back to the windshield, and things have heated even more.

But now... William isn't having it. He wheels his chair away from Roger, but Roger keeps screaming and following him around.

Then, the time freezes.

This is where it gets fuzzy.

William turns around and says something to Roger. He then wheels to the top of the stairs...

That's when my phone pings. *Ah, there you are, you little fucker!* The sound comes from under my sweater sitting on the passenger seat—I turn around for a split second, and when I gaze back at the window... something has shifted.

I catch the wheelchair flying down the stairs. Almost reaching the last step.

William thrusts out of the chair, his body flying until he lands on the floor.

Roger is standing at the top of the stairs, watching. That's it. Just standing there and watching.

He looks shocked—he must be. Or maybe just relieved.

He doesn't move for a few seconds, then finally strolls down the stairs.

At the bottom, William's body lies helplessly, splayed on the floor. Roger picks up his head, jostles it, and places his head close to William's mouth, as if he's trying to test if he's breathing. William is still not moving.

Roger stands up and paces the room back and forth, then he stops and pulls his phone out of his pocket.

He dials somebody; his mouth is moving a second later. Wish I could read his lips, but it's too far and I've never been good at it. His conversation is brief. He hangs up and puts his phone back in his pocket.

Roger takes one last look at William, turns around, and walks away from him.

I'm reeling. My eyes are wide in shock, and I'm scared about what's going to happen next. Is William going to live? I can only assume Roger called 911 to get William help as soon as possible. That's what any reasonable person would do.

But not Roger.

He is leaving the lobby and exiting into the rainy day. What the fuck?

He sees my car and waves in my direction, smiling, like nothing had happened. I'm taking deep breaths to calm myself. I don't witness murder every day, and of all days, it's when I'm already bleeding inside.

What about William?

Maybe he isn't dead after all?

He certainly looks dead to me. His body hasn't moved even an inch since he catapulted from his chair.

Roger runs toward my car, placing his hand on top of his head to protect himself from the rain. Good luck with that. By the time he arrives in my car, he's already soaked.

He opens the passenger door and slides into the seat.

"Hey." He gives me a quick kiss on my cheek. "Did you wait long?"

"No. No, I just arrived." I'm playing dumb. The last thing I want to do is admit what I just witnessed.

"Cool," he says as he takes a tissue out of a box and wipes his face with it. "I'm looking forward to a drink or two." He glances at me, his body tensing. "Shall we?"

Is he going to tell me about William? Anything at all?

I glance at his office building one more time—the lights are still on—and see no movement inside.

"Yeah, sure." I'm observing Roger. He's got that nervous tic reemerging.

He looks somewhere beyond the parking lot and then glances at me. "Were you here all by yourself waiting?"

"Umm. I think so. Pouring outside." I chuckle. "Most people don't want to be venturing out."

"Right." He imitates my chuckle. "Right."

There's a strange tension in the air. Roger gestures with his hand and raises his voice. "Let's go!"

And just like that—he's getting away with murder.

Being divorced is not the worst part of my life now.

The worst part is being broke as fuck.

Roger left me with nothing. Not a penny.

Irreconcilable differences are the reason listed for our marriage falling apart. I call it a euphemism for power and control.

I somehow doubt this is the law—the fact that we can't split Roger's assets—whatever is left of them. Roger is crafty. He was able to get a good lawyer on his side and rob me senseless. And I'm not quite in a position to hire someone worthy to fight Roger.

Sounds like a stroke of bad luck.

You can't put a smiley face on a tragedy and pretend everything is alright with the world. You can't stand outside during thunder, holding a metal pole, and not expect to be hit by lightning.

Roger hasn't forgiven me for my transgressions in our marriage, but he hides it behind diplomatic, nonsensical language. Irreconcilable differences. Just another way to save his reputation if there's any left.

But if someone told me I'd be living in North Las Vegas —which, statistically, it's known for high unemployment, brutal commutes, and a life none of us chose. After my divorce, I'd tell you to cram it. And yet, here I am: single, broke, and living in the place that has a reputation for breaking people who arrive already cracked.

It's noon. I'm sitting at my old computer, drinking my stale coffee, and staring at the dashboard of my checking account—$257.56 available. Shit! Money isn't everything, but when you're down to this, it feels like it is.

Let's be honest—I don't want to die poor and homeless. I don't even want to be broke.

When Roger's business was thriving, money was never a concern. I didn't work. I didn't need to. That was the deal. He told me he'd take care of everything, that I shouldn't worry about a thing. And for a while, I believed him.

Then, his business started to fail. The money tightened. The air between us changed. We sat at the kitchen table and talked about how to survive it.

"Maybe you should look for a job," he said.

His voice was calm and controlled.

But he disregarded the fact that I've been unemployable

for the majority of my adult life. It's not like I chose to be unemployable.

That ultimately became the problem in our marriage—my lack of a job, a career, proof that I was worth keeping. Not at the beginning. Never at the beginning. But years later, he acted as if this had always been my failure, as if I'd tricked him into carrying me.

It's not like I hadn't tried. I worked as a cashier at Walgreens until they replaced half the staff with self-checkout machines. Then I answered phones at a dentist's office, reminding people of appointments they still managed to miss. They let me go quietly, like I'd never been there at all.

Now I'm here. Jobless. Still.

I log out of my bank account and take a sip of coffee from the table. It's cold. I spit it back into the cup.

"Ugh."

The house I am staying in is one bedroom, one bath, wedged into a neighborhood that howls at night: dogs, people, sometimes both. The house is old in the worst way. Popcorn ceilings. Thick brown carpet everywhere, even in the bathroom. It's the place that drains whatever joy you walked in with.

The house I grew up in wasn't any nicer, but the neighborhood was decent and safe. I lived with my parents until I was ten, then moved in with my Aunt Susan in Seattle.

The houses here sit so close together I once caught my

neighbor brushing his teeth, staring straight ahead, unaware he was being watched.

I go to the kitchen and brew fresh coffee. Coffee helps. Coffee pretends things are normal. I'll need it if I'm going to look for a job.

What kind of job can a thirty-two year old with a high school diploma and no real experience get? Retail. Phones. Smiling until my face hurts. That diploma—I could shove it up my ass.

I interviewed at Macy's last week. The manager was thrilled with my "previous retail experience." I felt nothing. If he calls, I'll take the job. Of course I will.

Until then, I occupy my time scrolling through my phone, playing games until the sun disappears. Even doing nothing feels exhausting now.

I SLEEP IN, like I always do, and swing my legs out of bed.

The room smells stale—old carpet and bleach—and it puts me in a foul mood before the day even starts. It's quite a demotion from living in the upscale neighborhood, Instrada, that bustled with restaurants, shopping, and people who didn't know what to do with all their money.

I don't know anybody here. Not even a next-door neighbor. I keep to myself, because God knows I won't be here long.

Sleepy-eyed, I stare out the window, first see my Jeep sitting in the cracked driveway. The only useful thing in my life. The day is sunny and beautiful, but it doesn't help lift my mood.

I'm about to walk away from the window when the mailman approaches my mailbox. It's funny—when I think about it, opening the mail was always my job when I was married to Roger. He let me handle the bills—the electricity, the gardener, the pool boy—and it felt easy then, even satisfying, because I never had to worry. When the money got tight, and we started budgeting every dollar, Roger took over. And the strangest part of all was that he wouldn't let me anywhere near the mail after that.

One thing to look forward to, I guess, is opening up my mail again. Something to be said about control... even with the smallest things.

The mailman looks like he's in a hurry as he opens my mailbox, shoves in a few envelopes, and slams the door shut. He doesn't look up in my direction for me to see his face, but I can tell he's mad about something.

Once he's far enough down the street, I step outside and walk to the mailbox. I can't remember the last time I received anything that mattered. Just bills. Junk. Envelopes that go straight into the recycling without being opened. Even so, there's a pull to it—the hope that one of them might mean something.

I peer inside the mailbox. Three envelopes. One of them

sits on top, clean and white, not trying too hard. It looks intentional.

I take it out. It's addressed to me. Rachel Browning. Handwritten.

That alone is enough to set my pulse off. People don't write names by hand unless they want your attention. I tell myself that's a good thing. I let myself believe it might be. I've applied to a number of jobs, maybe it's a response to one of them. I feel hopeful.

I hurry back inside, flipping the envelope in my hand, eyes fixed on it, and shut the door behind me.

Before I open my mail, I run to the kitchen to grab a paring knife. The stamp looks clean, with no ink on it, so I'd better peel it off and save it in case I need it later.

I open the wrong drawer and find old photos scattered on top—mostly of Roger and me when we first met. In the photos, we're always looking at each other, smiling, in love. If someone had to describe us, they'd say we were swans: graceful, inseparable, together forever.

That was when Roger believed trauma was temporary. Harmless. Something without a spine, something you could decapitate and leave behind.

But that's not how it works. I tried to tell him.

As I flip through the photos, I stop in my tracks.

A photo of my young mom.

"How did this get here?" I whisper.

She looks beautiful. Those big green eyes — I will never

forget how she looked at me lovingly. She wore a T-shirt and overalls in the photo—you can almost see sweat accumulated on her forehead—looks like she just finished a long painting job around the house.

This was before her face was mutilated. Beaten to a pulp. The woman in the photograph doesn't resemble what the crime turned her into.

Her mutilated face—that's how she was buried. It was practically nonexistent.

My hands shiver and my heart flutters with anxiety.

I drop it back in the drawer and slam it shut.

I find the paring knife in the top drawer. I painstakingly remove the Forever stamp from the envelope and put the stamp in the drawer. For worse days to come.

I go back to the living room, clear a small space on the couch, sit, and tear the envelope open. Inside is a single sheet of paper, folded into thirds. I smooth it out and read.

Dear Rachel,

We are inviting you for an exclusive stay at a luxury hotel for a chance to win $6 million.

My eyes snag on the number. Six million dollars. That's not a gift. Sounds more like a reality TV show gone wrong.

No one offers that kind of money for something as simple as staying at a hotel. There's always a catch. I keep reading, waiting for it to show itself.

But here's the catch. In order to win the money, you will have no access to the outside world for thirty days. No phones, no computers, no Internet. All you may take with you are your personal garments, hygiene items, and five books.

Do you think you can stand up to the challenge? If so, email us your brief biography and a video only one minute long, telling us about yourself. Convince us that you should be the one to get this opportunity.

The deadline is July 30.

We will choose the winner soon!

Good luck!

I scoff. It reads like a scam. No one gives away that kind of money for a stay in a luxury hotel. It sounds like a dare rich people cooked up when they got bored.

I tell myself that and almost believe it. Almost.

What if it's real? What if this is someone trying to balance the scales, paying penance with a fortune they'll never miss?

I hate how quickly my brain works. Pros and cons. Mostly pros. Six million dollars would buy breathing room. No more staring at the electric bill, wondering when the lights will go out. No more lying awake over rent.

The downside is obvious. I quit. I crack. I walk out halfway through because I can't stand the isolation, the silence, the pressure of being alone that long.

Then again—Roger and I just divorced. Maybe thirty days alone isn't punishment. Maybe it's exactly what I need. Time to sit with my choices. Figure out who I am without him. Decide what to do with a future that suddenly comes with commas. To heal in solitude.

I drop the paper onto the floor and check my phone. July 25. Five days until the deadline.

No time to waste.

I dash to the bathroom, stop in front of the mirror, and reach for my makeup bag.

TWO

RACHEL BROWNING

After I finish dolling myself up, I move into the living room and scan the space like I'm seeing it through someone else's eyes. I choose the most presentable corner—the couch, a neutral painting on the wall, and a plant. On second thought, maybe not the plant. It's half dead, like me, and begging for attention. From a distance, it passes.

I prop my phone against the large candle on the coffee table and switch the camera on. The screen stares back at me. I check my reflection. The makeup gives me just enough spark to look alive, and the low-cut dress does what it's supposed to do. Presentable. Approachable. Someone worth six million dollars. I purse my lips, smooth my hair, and nod at myself like we've agreed.

I smile. It doesn't reach my eyes.

"Hi, my name is Rachel Browning."

The words hit the air and die there. I freeze, staring at my own face on the screen, my mind suddenly empty.

"Oh, fuck."

I stop the video and delete it before I can overthink it. A long sigh escapes me. This shouldn't be hard. It's just talk. But my chest feels tight, like I've forgotten how to introduce myself without attaching someone else to my name.

I set the phone back on the table, straighten my shoulders, and hit RECORD again.

"My name is Rachel Browning. I'm thirty-two years old. Recently single." I pause, then continue. "I grew up in Seattle, but I moved to Las Vegas in my early twenties. I've always been fascinated by the city."

I add a small laugh, light and harmless. People like that. Judges like that.

Not the actual ugly history. Not the ugly childhood. The things we witness. Nobody wants to hear that. Like they're going to catch it like it's a virus.

"Right now, I'm in between jobs, which means I have the time and flexibility to commit. No kids. No husband."

I stop the recording and sit there, thinking. That there's no one depending on me should help me, right? No small children to leave behind. No spouse counting the days until I come home. And Roger—he's not my problem anymore. Whatever mess he's made of his life, it doesn't get to follow me into this.

I press RECORD again.

"Why would I be a suitable candidate?" I ask, leaning in slightly. "I love adventure. I've traveled to Spain, Germany, and Italy. I've visited the Grand Canyon—"

The lie slips out smoothly. I've never been to any of those places. I wanted to go. Roger always said we would. He had a real talent for making promises that never happened.

"And more importantly," I continue, "I believe I can do this. This feels like the right moment. After a divorce, you either shrink or you reinvent yourself. I want the time and space to figure out who I am and what I want next. And what better place than a hotel? What better time than now?"

I smile again, wider this time, and end strong: "I hope you pick me."

When I watch the video back, I tilt my head from side to side, surprised. I look convincing. Confident. Like someone who hasn't spent the last year watching her life collapse in slow motion.

The invitation letter is somewhere in the room. I dig through the couch cushions until I find it folded between the pillows. I open a new email, carefully type in the address from the letter, and attach the video. I add a short bio, typing slowly so I don't misspell my name.

Rachel Browning, 32. Recently single and eager to begin a new adventure. Thank you for your consideration.

A small giggle escapes me. I can't believe I actually did it.

I'm not stupid. I know how the world works. People don't just hand over millions out of kindness. But the effort was minimal. Ten minutes. Makeup. A video. An email. If ten minutes is all I stand to lose, then so be it.

Because, what's the alternative?

I've never been one of those lucky people who get picked. Not once in my adult life have I emerged a winner. That probably has something to do with my childhood—messy in the way most people pretend doesn't matter unless they're lying to themselves.

Aunt Susan did an okay job raising me under the circumstances. She had no kids, and never wanted them, so I'm sure she took me in reluctantly, promising herself to do a bare minimum raising me. She drove hundreds of miles to summon me the day my dad was locked up for good—life sentence, no chance of parole. She was the only blood relative willing to take me in and do a half-decent job of pretending things were normal.

But she could never get the scene from my childhood out of my head.

I shake my head to dislodge the memory.

What if the invitation is real? What if not everything is a scam? What if, just this once, something works out?

I sit there for a moment, letting the idea settle. I don't need certainty. I just need a chance.

I hit SEND. The soft whoosh of the email leaving feels louder than it should. Final.

I smile and murmur to myself. "You only live once."

THREE
FELECIA MEBANE
ONE YEAR EARLIER – JUNE 20, 8:01 PM

I turn on the engine and put the gear in reverse.

Roger looks around the parking lot—still void of people.

Though, as I follow his eyes, my gaze lands on a car that looks just like Roger's tucked in the far corner of the lot. Can't be his, right? He said he had it at the repair shop unless I somehow misheard him. With the sheet of rain pelting down on my car, it's possible I am imagining things. Besides, why can't there be another Audi that looks just like Roger's?

He's awfully quiet. Just sitting in the passenger seat, looking pensive. His eyes, big and wide, dart to the building. His eyebrows stitch together. Not a peep comes out of his mouth.

You can't call Roger a quiet, keeps to-himself guy. He likes to talk. He's usually a chatterbox, filling silence with stories, complaints, jokes, noise. About his business and clients, how demanding all of it is, but I know he's loving it. Roger loves to be needed.

But now? Nothing. Just the rhythmic tap of his fingers against the door.

We pull out of the parking lot, turning right onto the nearly empty street. I'm as tense as a stick, navigating the roads in darkness and rain, my mind scrambling to process whatever happened just minutes ago.

If William is dead, now is the chance to turn around and do something about it. I guess the only way to test a conscience is to act now.

Roger's leg moves restlessly, and it's getting my attention more than I want. I do my best not to pay attention to the movement. I need to pay razor-sharp attention to the road.

Minutes go by, but Roger doesn't say a word. He's tapping his fingers on the door, looking through the window, the rain pelting down with a vengeance.

Despite myself, I turn on the radio to divert the tension in the car. Ozzy Osborn, *Mama I'm Coming Home*, plays on. Damn, this song always tears me up. Not now. And that means something. I'm too tense to feel sadness.

The streets are nearly empty.

Streetlights blur into long yellow streaks on the wet pavement, and the windshield wipers fight to keep up with the rain. I grip the steering wheel a little tighter, every muscle in my body wound like a coil.

Roger still hasn't spoken.

I steal a glance at him. His jaw is tense. His eyes are distant. Haunted, like he's still trying to process what he saw minutes ago.

What we both saw minutes ago. I turn off the radio.

"How's your day been?" I break the silence.

He nods. "Fine." He glances at me with a quick smile.

"Just fine?" I tease.

"Nothing special." He pinches his forehead with his forefinger and a thumb. Like he doesn't want to engage. A tic appears on his face. It's the small things that give him away.

While I'm driving, I do my best to keep calm. Have to be careful not to get into an accident in this calamity. Have to keep calm for different reasons. Roger keeps his eyes on the road, too, like that's going to make a difference. Like that's going to keep us safe from the slippery roads and invisible horizon.

That's Roger for you—always on the lookout like he's a fucking savior.

It's probably one reason Roger has said nothing about William. Just imagine my reaction if Roger said these words: I killed William. And me veering off the road, killing us both.

I certainly wouldn't take it well. He probably knows it would cause a knee-jerk reaction and maybe we'd end up in a ditch, dead.

Killing William is one thing. Killing both of us turns violence into intention.

The rain intensifies, hammering the car roof like a drum.

The world outside feels swallowed by the storm, but the tension inside the car is worse—a suffocating weight pressing down on my chest.

I clear my throat, trying to find something—anything—to break the oppressive silence. I could turn the radio back on, but that won't change Roger acting aloof.

So, I drive.

We pass the empty sidewalks. The darkened shops. The Strip, where some fools stagger down the street, tourists drunk on cheap thrills and poor decisions.

By the time we reach the restaurant, my hands are trembling on the wheel.

Roger still hasn't said a word.

FOUR
RACHEL BROWNING
A WEEK LATER

I never thought I'd say it, but missing my life with Roger creeps up on me.

Not in a way that breaks my heart in two and tears up my eyes. I miss the familiarity that's now gone. The little habits we had—watching TV until late, chatting over coffee in the morning, fighting over trivial things—those are the things that shaped our marriage, for better or for worse.

It's complicated. Losing a person is not something that ever connotes a happy ending. Even if the person made your life hell, you'd still need to take time to adjust to the new life you're handed without them. Mourn over the loss, whatever the fuck it was.

I've heard of the term Stockholm syndrome. Our marriage wasn't like that. It's not like I was the victim, and he preyed on my weakness. It's that he failed to follow through on the vows: for better or for worse. When things started to crack—when things turned worse—so did his patience. Empathy? That's for suckers, not people like Roger.

Now that I'm wasting time away, with no real prospects on the horizon, even those pointless fights are more meaningful now.

I've neglected myself. I haven't worked out in weeks. I haven't seen any of my friends. I didn't even get the retail job I interviewed for recently. And what's worst—I have missed a couple of sessions with my therapist.

Strange things have crept into my head. The nightmares are back. I haven't had them in years, not since I learned how to pretend I was fine.

It's always the same one. I'm trapped in a tunnel shaped like a semicircle, smooth and narrow, the walls pressing in close enough that I can feel them breathing. There's no exit. No place to turn around. Just forward.

I'm running, my footsteps echoing too loudly, too fast. Someone is behind me. Not just a single person. A bunch.

I never see their faces, only the shadows stretching ahead of them, crawling up the walls like a warning I'm too late to heed. I push harder, lungs burning, legs shaking, knowing it won't matter.

Then I reach the middle of the tunnel. The exact center. That's when I realize I'm not alone up ahead. There's someone waiting for me there. Calm. Patient. Blocking the only way forward.

I stop. I turn. Too late.

There's someone on the other side, blocking my path.

They close in from both sides, and I'm wedged between them, ambushed in that narrow space, pressed tight, unable to move. I know what's coming before it happens. I know this is where they'll kill me.

I always wake up just before it finishes, scared, with a pounding heart and a parched mouth. And no matter how many times I tell myself it's just a dream, the panic lingers—because some part of me understands the truth.

I'm not running away from them.

I'm running toward something I can't avoid.

Life without Roger feels unfamiliar, like I've stepped into a version of my life that doesn't quite fit. My life before Roger was in shambles—trying to get by, living off government assistance. Not very sexy, right? Roger came along and knew about my life but didn't seem to care at first.

The worst parts don't show up during the day. They come at night. They slip into my sleep and replay themselves as nightmares, distorted but relentless.

My therapist used to tell me these dreams came from trauma. My mom. The way her life ended tragically.

But now, there's another reason for these very same dreams: Roger.

I wake up already exhausted, carrying a fear I can't explain. And the strangest part is how familiar it feels, like my body remembers something my mind refuses to name.

What's worse?

The dreams don't feel like they're about Roger at all. They feel like alarm bells. Like a signal that worse days are coming.

Now that he's no longer around, there is a lot more silence. I am not used to it.

Silence is a strange thing. It presses in, loud and unforgiving, filling every corner of the house. I used to think I liked quiet. Now it feels like something I have to relearn, like riding a bike or swimming after years out of the water—muscle memory gone, confidence shot.

I'm not good at this. Not at being alone for this long. The stillness makes me restless, sharpens my thoughts until they cut. So, I turn on the television and crank the volume, not because I'm watching it, but because I need proof that something else is alive in the room. Anything.

I plop on the couch and watch the news—there's always something terrible happening locally and in the world, so I switch to another channel. HGTV. Fancy houses on the screen—they remind me of what I've lost, so I keep changing the channels until I settle on National Geographic. Whales and the ocean.

I'll take animals over people any day.

I walk to the kitchenette and make myself a peanut butter and jelly sandwich. Since Roger and I divorced, I've lost several pounds already. A lack of appetite will do it to you. But I still need to eat and live.

My phone rings, and I stop in my tracks.

That's another thing. My phone doesn't ring as much anymore. Even Julie has been too busy herding kids at a summer camp and preparing the curriculum for the next school year.

I stop what I am doing, my face scrunching at the sound of the phone. It's ringing as if it's sending a warning. Insistent. Loud.

I wipe my wet hands on my sweatpants and make a beeline to the living room to get my phone.

Unknown number. A video call.

I slide the call open and see a middle-aged man staring right at me.

He smiles and gives a small wave. "Hey, Rachel."

He knows my name. Obviously. I have never seen him. Nothing about him looks familiar.

My eyes squint. "Who are you?"

He smiles. "My name is Josh. I'm calling to let you know you've been selected for a chance to win six million dollars."

My eyes bulge in surprise. "Wait. What?"

If the letter seemed like a scam, this video call seems more like a dream I just stepped into. It's like a miracle happens out of the blue, and you don't know what hit you first.

Josh keeps smiling. A friendly face indeed. Real.

"We received your short bio and video the other day, and we loved it." Josh's smile does not disappear. But then it does abruptly. "We're very sorry about your recent divorce. Been there, done that."

His words still sound like a scratched tape, like something I'm still fine-tuning so I can hear better. *You've been selected for a chance to win six million dollars.* I've never been selected for anything good in my life.

Besides, until this call, I'd forgotten all about it. I must've pushed it out of my mind, the skeptic in me certain nothing like this ever actually happens.

"Are you sure?" I ask.

Josh nods. "I'm positive. We received over a thousand applications, and yours seems to be the most compelling. No job. Recent divorce. A hungry sense of adventure." He pauses and leans forward, and I can see all the features of his face up-close. "And if I can be honest, you're easy on the eyes." He chuckles.

I'm used to compliments, but my good looks shouldn't matter. They probably don't. Maybe Josh is just making small talk. Maybe he's nervous.

He isn't unattractive. Short, wavy brown hair. Blue eyes. A jawline sharp enough to suggest confidence—or something rehearsed. He has the type of face that makes you look twice, then wonder why you did.

"Thank you," I smile back.

His compliment reminds me when Roger and I went out for dinner or drinks, people noticed. They looked. Roger noticed too. He knew men and women were checking me out, and it drove him crazy. It became another fault line in our marriage. He couldn't stand my being the center of attention. And he couldn't bring himself to be proud of me.

"What do I need to do?" I let out a nervous chuckle and tuck a strand of hair behind my ear.

"Good question." Josh says. "As the letter mentioned, you're going to spend thirty days in a hotel room, on your own." He coughs and looks to his right as if thinking. Then his eyes rest on me again. "For thirty days, you will not be allowed to talk to the outside world, which means you can't have your phone or your computer."

No phone. No computer. It's not like I am talking to anyone now. What difference would it make?

I nod. "I'm okay with that."

"Good. Good." Josh says. "You are, however, allowed to bring books with you."

That sounds like a little piece of good news, but the bad news is I don't remember the last time I read a book. "What about magazines? Is that okay?"

"Of course." Josh is all smiles. "If you enjoy playing Sudoku or crossword puzzles, bring those, too. Trust me. You'll need them."

His last sentence is laced with a dark undertone. I don't like the way he sounds.

Trust me. You'll need them.

What does he mean by it?

The only thing it could mean is that whatever I'll be up against won't be easy.

But things seem to be cementing more and sound closer to the truth, as we further our plans.

"What... what happens if I can't get through it?"

Josh tilts his head, bulges his eyes. "That's certainly a possibility. If, let's say, you decide the experiment isn't for you and you can no longer carry on with it, you just go home... as simple as that. And of course, that means you won't get a penny." He shrugs.

My mind is churning. What if this thing ends up being worse than it sounds?

"How did your previous contestants fare?"

Josh fidgets in his seat. "There aren't any previous contestants. You're the very first one. So, bear with us. It's the first time we're organizing all this."

"It is?" A pang of nervousness washes over me. What if things go horribly wrong? They have no prior experience to draw from when handling something like this. Being the first one makes me feel like a guinea pig.

"But don't worry." It's like Josh reads my mind. "Like I said, you can always quit and go home if you can't continue."

Josh knows very little about me. Sure, I will divorce my husband if both of us are miserable, but I'm not a quitter. Never have been. Certainly not when $6 million are at stake. This is only to say that I will stubbornly continue with the mission even if it kills me.

"Let me ask." My mind is churning. "Are there any other conditions I need to be aware of?"

"Another great question." Josh chuckles. "While you are not allowed to leave the hotel parameters, you can walk around inside the hotel, go to the restaurant or bar by the lobby. Also—while you're not allowed to speak to your family members and friends, you're allowed to talk to strangers who pass by the hotel."

While Josh is speaking, I feel like being in a trance. He sounds like he's reading from a piece of paper or like he has rehearsed his speech so many times. He pauses for a few seconds, and a whisper of a different voice comes through my phone speaker.

Who is that? Is Josh with someone else in the room? I can't even tell where he is. His background is all white, like it could be just a fake background or there is a white wall behind him. I don't have a chance to ask if he's with someone in the room. He continues with the guidelines.

"There won't be a physical phone in the room, so you won't be able to dial anyone." He pauses and clears his throat. "Not even the hotel staff."

I feel unease in my chest. "Not even the hotel staff? What if there's an emergency?"

"I was about to get to that." Josh's voice gets deeper as our conversation continues. "There is a camera installed in the room, and if you need something, you will need to communicate using your hands. Because obviously we won't be able to hear you."

"With my hands? How will you know what I mean?" I panic, thinking immediately about how all of it could go wrong from the very beginning.

I wonder if I should back out of the whole deal. It sounds too far-fetched and like a fairy tale that doesn't end well.

"The instructions will be left in the room. We will automatically drop off three meals a day and snacks, and you will have two-time slots to get out of the room and walk around." He smiles as he did at the beginning of the call. "So, as you see, it doesn't seem as bad."

"I don't know..." I whisper.

Josh chimes in with excitement, "And the best part, of course, on day thirty, we deposit six million dollars into your bank account. You walk away from the hotel with no strings attached. You will be a free woman. And rich, to boot."

His smile lingers for a long second, but his look seems hollow.

If I'm skeptical, I'm just as curious, if not more. "Where's the hotel?"

"The hotel?" Josh rubs his chin with his index finger. "It's a five-star hotel. It's The Four Seasons in the heart of Boston. And if you decide to do this, you will need to leave tonight."

A sudden bolt of fear hits me.

I don't like hearing I have a couple of hours to get ready and head to the airport. Gives me instant anxiety.

It's akin to a couple you barely know inviting you to their wedding the same day—except you don't own a dress, you don't have money for a gift, and no one seems to care how impossible that is. It's rude. Thoughtless. Almost deliberate.

Josh says the experiment starts tomorrow. August 1. Which means today—this day—is already over in his mind. The last day of July, written off like a receipt you don't bother keeping. And if I want to be part of whatever comes next, I'd better move quickly—pack my life into a suitcase and pretend this all makes sense.

Let me be clear—I don't like the word he uses: *experiment*. It settles in my chest and refuses to move, making me re-evaluate every promise he's already made.

Still, I force myself into motion.

My bedroom looks like a crime scene—my things are scattered across the floor. Clothes. Old purses. The debris of a marriage I meant to clean out months ago and never did. I always thought I'd have more time. Turns out motivation doesn't arrive until the clock is running out.

I tell myself this is temporary. That, once I'm rich, I'll pay someone else to sort through the wreckage. Someone with gloves and no memories. Someone who doesn't care what any of it meant.

Maybe it's the blessing in disguise. But still...

FIVE
RACHEL BROWNING

I glance back at Josh's face on the screen. "Tonight?" I ask. "Isn't that... too soon?"

He rubs the back of his neck. A nervous tic, or maybe just a habit. "The suite is only available for this time window," he says. "Thirty days. Starting tomorrow. Well—tonight. Technically." He clears his throat. "And besides, it's never too soon to have fun."

He says it lightly, like that should reassure me.

It doesn't.

I look around the room again. The same piles. The same walls. Freedom, apparently, looks like clutter and regret. Some people would feel lucky. I don't.

"Okay," I say, surprising myself. "I'll do it."

Anything is better than staying here, staring at the TV until midnight and pretending that counts as a life.

Josh doesn't waste time.

An Uber will take me to the airport. A man named Charlie will buy my plane ticket. In Boston, a cab will be waiting. Paid for. Easy. Seamless.

Who would say no to this?

"You can keep your phone while you travel," he adds. "But when you arrive at the hotel, you'll leave it with Susan at the front desk. You won't get it back until day thirty."

Thirty days without a phone. The words hit like a physical blow.

I glance at my watch. Almost eleven. "What time is the Uber coming?"

Josh scans the room behind his camera, as if searching for a clock. "A couple of hours," he says. "That's all you'll need. Anything you forget—we'll buy it."

Of course they will.

"Any last questions?"

I shake my head. Slowly. "No." I can't think of any other questions now that this plan has hijacked my entire day.

"Good luck, Rachel," he says, smiling wide. "I'll see you on day thirty—with the money."

Then the screen goes dark.

The silence afterward is deafening.

Two hours sounds generous until you realize what it's counting down to. This isn't packing for a trip. It's packing for disappearance.

I drag a suitcase out of the bedroom closet, the one Roger and I used when we were still pretending. Too big. Too full of ghosts. I shove it back and grab a smaller bag instead. Clothes. Makeup. Toothbrush. Nothing sentimental. Nothing that would hurt to lose.

My stomach twists. Nerves, maybe. Or instinct.

I picture the hotel. The Four Seasons. I look it up anyway. Immaculate and perfect. A place where nothing bad is supposed to happen.

I remind myself: this is voluntary. I can walk away. No one is forcing me.

That thought calms me. A little.

When the bag is packed, I sit on the couch and wait. My mind races, checking and rechecking an invisible list. Josh said they'd buy whatever I forgot. I cling to that like a lifeline.

Soon, the Uber will be here.

I take one last walk through the house. The junk. The noise. The stale air of a life already over.

Staying another night would be unbearable.

I don't hesitate.

I can't wait to get out.

SIX
RACHEL BROWNING

Mom used to say panic is your worst enemy. Panic never fixes anything. It only makes things worse, twisting everything into a spiral that pulls you down until there's nothing left to grab. If you don't slow yourself down, if you don't take that breath, you fall. Hard. And when you fall, you get hurt.

I take a slow, steadying breath in the back of the Uber. Exhale. Inhale again. Repeat. My mind ticks off the checklist: ID, wallet, phone, toothbrush, charger, clothes for a month. Everything is packed. Everything I need. There's only one thing left: call Julie. Let her know what I'm doing.

The periphery of the city is an unimpressive wasteland. Nothing happens around here until you get to the Strip. I can't say I'll miss it, but, still, I stare through the window and take it all in.

The Uber doesn't need to fight traffic. Twenty minutes to the airport, maybe less. Long enough to make the call.

I pull my phone out and dial. Rings. Rings. Rings. But Julie doesn't pick up. Of course not. Always too busy. Julie is my best friend, but, unlike me, she has three small kids that keep her busy and stressed out all the time. I try not to burden her with my problems, though, I feel she should know what I'm up to the next month. I don't want to add more stress to her life in case she tries to reach me only to get no responses.

I glance at the driver. He's focused on the road, but I can feel the weight of the possibility that he's listening. I decide against leaving a voicemail. Some things are better kept to yourself. Some things are better left unspoken until you're ready—or until it's too late to stop them from happening.

Maybe not reaching Julie is a blessing in disguise. Maybe fate doesn't want me talking right now.

At the airport, Charlie finds me before I can even catch my bearings. No text. No call. No coordination. Somehow, he just... knows. And when I see him, I almost laugh at how absurd it feels: a heavyset man, red beard, wool beret in a hundred-degree city. He could be a hitman in some low-budget thriller.

He extends a hand. "Here's your plane ticket," he says. Raspy, deep, steady. There's a deliberate calm to him that doesn't comfort me—it unnerves me. "It's one way to Boston. When you finish your stay, you'll have enough to buy a ticket anywhere."

A quick, almost imperceptible smile flickers across his face and vanishes.

"Thanks," I say, keeping my tone neutral.

"You have your ID?"

I nod, tap my pockets. "Yes."

He points. "Security is that way. Your plane boards in forty minutes." He digs into his pocket and hands me an envelope. "A little something for lunch."

I peek inside. Twenty-dollar bills. Enough. How does he know I'm practically penniless? My stomach tightens. These people know too much. And I haven't told them a thing.

"Well... I'll be on my way. Good luck."

And just like that, he's gone. I do what he said—security, gate, tickets—and as soon as I lose sight of him, something shifts in me. Excitement, tinged with fear, courses through my veins. This trip—this choice—could change everything. Or it could destroy me.

What if it doesn't?

What if this is all a lie, a trap I've walked into blindly?

I shove the thought aside. Now is not the time for panic. Not here. Not yet.

The plane fills slowly, the door clicks shut, and flight attendants walk the aisles with casual, practiced smiles. They look serene. I clutch my purse, knuckles white. The window seat is mine. Half of the plane is empty. The man in front of me leans back and snores softly.

I can't sleep. Flying always reminds me of the early days

with Roger. Newly married, wide-eyed, reckless. He had this look in his eyes, a tension I didn't understand at the time. Something he kept hidden, maybe even from himself. Fast-forward a few years, and he says the marriage is no longer working.

That's when everything went to hell. Now the reason I am here, on this plane, on my way to Boston, hoping for a better chance at life.

Six and a half hours in the air. Uneventful.

Boston's Logan Airport greets me with a cold, quiet darkness. A cab whisks me away to The Four Seasons, windows reflecting the city lights like scattered diamonds. Traffic is light. Fifteen minutes, and I'm there.

The hotel strikes me as odd. Triangular, nestled perfectly between three streets. The Bermuda Triangle flashes in my mind—a place where things disappear without a trace. Strange thought, but fitting.

The building itself is pristine, expensive. Rooms starting at nearly $400 a night. When Roger and I traveled, never once did we stay somewhere like this. Never. And yet... here I am.

I take a deep breath, the air flooding my lungs like oxygen after a long dive. This is my chance. Thirty days, six million dollars, a life I could never have imagined.

The cab pulls away. Now, it's just me standing there alone, staring at the hotel like it's the last thing I'll ever see on earth.

Thirty days. Six million dollars. A challenge I can rise to.

A smile forms, tentative but real. *You can do this. You've survived worse. You will survive this.*

And somewhere in the back of my mind, a small, cautious voice whispers: or maybe you won't.

I chuckle, shaking it off. For tonight, I will try to believe in the first possibility.

PART 2

By the time we get to the restaurant, the rain has stopped, and Roger still hasn't said a word about William.

If there was any trust left in Roger, it's gone. A sliver of hope flickers anyway. Maybe Roger will say something at dinner.

We walk through the parking lot, my mind still rewinding the earlier images. They stick like a bad movie.

I still think he pushed him over the edge and watched him roll down the stairs, pretending it was an accident. It's one thing to stage it, but to flee afterward—that's the most cowardly thing I've ever seen Roger do. His calmness is eerie.

For me, his ability to kill coldly and hide it makes me want to stay vigilant. I need to watch his every move from now on. Just another thing to track.

Maybe he's preparing for admission. Maybe—after

dinner—he'll go to the police station and turn himself in. Sometimes regret catches up later, once pride wears off.

In the back of my mind, I do consider the possibility that he didn't kill him. After all, I turned around to look for my phone, and when I looked back at the building, William was nearly at the bottom of the stairs. Sure, maybe Roger didn't push him. It's very possible William tried to get away from Roger and, in the haze, somehow wheeled his chair further than he should have, caught the edge of the top stair and went flying down.

Maybe William is fine. Alive! Maybe he will be okay.

If he's not, it's the aftermath that rattled me.

The way Roger watched him roll, the way he glided down the stairs as if this were some game—careless, almost delighted.

Roger hasn't said a word on our way to the restaurant. Maybe he's looking for the best moment to break the news. That's the hope.

We go to the same restaurant, where we usually sit in a corner, away from people's hungry eyes. Where Roger's clients don't dine. So, of course, Roger's preference. It's like he wants to hide me from the world, and I never say no even though it makes me feel smaller.

The hostess knows us well.

She ushers us to the corner, holding two menus, handing them over when we sit down like they are gold medals.

Roger doesn't look at me. Not once. He sits back in his

chair, hands folded loosely on the table, shoulders relaxed. Somewhere between the car and this table, he's found his calm, and it makes my unease sharpen.

When the waitress arrives at our table, Roger orders a double martini. I watch him, measuring every move.

Something shifts.

There's nervous energy about him when he flips the menu back and forth, back and forth, rubs his stubble as he reads from the menu.

"Geez, will they ever add any new entrees?" His voice is edgy. He sounds borderline pissed. It can't be the menu, can it?

"It's a family restaurant." I say. "They probably try to make it simple. Love it or leave it."

He glances at me, gives me a small smile, his eyes not quite matching it.

"Right." He says.

I look through the window; the street is soaked by the rain. My thoughts run to William's body. It's just lying there on the floor until someone finds him. Is that the plan? Did Roger set it up so that someone would come to the office and find the helpless William and call 911?

Maybe that was the call Roger made. Asked someone to stop by the office only to find William.

When the ambulance arrives, everything will look like an accident. Oh, William must have fallen at least a couple of hours ago, dead for at least an hour; the autopsy will reveal. I can imagine the narrative: Roger left the office shortly before, said goodbye to William, and went to dinner.

Perfect alibi. And even if not perfect, there's no apparent proof Roger did anything to cause William's fall.

Except there's one thing.

Roger doesn't know I saw half of it.

WHILE WAITING FOR FOOD, Roger is already on his second double martini. I'm nursing my Diet Coke, observing Roger's shoulders relax. The alcohol is taking the edge off a bit.

"How was your day?" he asks.

"Not bad." I'm short, curt. I'm expecting the genuine conversation to begin. Confession of sorts.

Something else comes out of Roger's mouth: "I've been meaning to tell you..." he pauses and takes a slurp of his drink. He lets out a gigantic sigh to show just how much he's enjoying his drink, but I think he's just curtailing his anxiety. "The business is not going well."

That's what he wants to tell me? Not about Willam?

"You hinted at it the other day." I say.

He runs his hand over his bald head. Roger usually wears caps to hide his baldness, but today, he's somehow letting loose. When I first met Roger, he had a full head of hair... and now... he has said the constant stress has grated on him and caused the hair loss.

Not what I expected to hear. My forehead wrinkles. "Why?"

His business?

Interior design.

It's his passion, his life, his blood. He and William made a name for themselves—some of the best in the country—but now I wonder if his decline in business has anything to do with what happened tonight.

"Blame it on technology." He shakes his head, rolls his eyes. "They don't need interior designers like they did before AI."

"AI?" I ask, incredulous.

He nods. "Artificial intelligence. Nowadays, everyone slaps photos in the app and lets AI do the work." He scoffs. "Fucking hell."

Roger is not a quitter. Hearing him say these words sounds like he's given up already. And that makes it even more suspicious of what Roger has become over the past several months.

"But I'm sure your business will continue, right?"

Roger cocks his head, makes a sympathetic face. "Felecia. Please. Don't sound like you've been living under a rock. Times are changing."

Cocky bastard.

"I don't think that's a fair statement..."

Roger doesn't seem to listen. He keeps looking down at his phone. It's sitting on the table, next to his unused napkin. Is he waiting for a phone call? Someone to tell him William is dead?

Roger already knows William is dead. He's pretending he doesn't, because now I'm certain that he pushed him down the stairs and killed him.

"Okay, and what does that mean as far as your business? Future prospects..." my words trail off. Fear prickles under my skin. I can already feel the answer won't be something I want to hear.

He grabs his martini glass and sips, then places it gently on the table. He simply shrugs. "I don't know. But I'll tell you —no more fancy clothes and expensive trips."

His eyes lift to mine, steady and unblinking. "You know I love you. But from here on out, Felecia... it's just survival." He takes a sip of his martini and looks into the distance.

And in that moment, I know—he's not just talking about the business.

He's talking about me.

"Welcome to the Four Seasons! My name's Scott," a young man says, stepping toward me as I climb out of the taxi. The air is chilly compared to the Vegas pressure cooker during the day. I sigh deeply and feel reborn. A mix of the sea, car exhaust, and humidity is in the air—and despite the unsettling unfamiliarity, I enjoy it all.

I spin around to take in my surroundings and look up at the sky. When Roger was hopeful about life, he'd always say, the sky's the limit. He'd preach like he's got all the answers in the world, but for the first time, I feel his advice. Nothing ventured, nothing gained. What's the point of living if we don't spice up our lives?

"Let me help you." Scott bends to lift my luggage.

Scott is a large man—broad-shouldered, at least 6'2", built like he belongs on a football team. For him, carrying my bag would be like pushing a feather through the air.

"Oh, you don't have to," I tell him, though the bag is light enough to drag myself.

"No worries," he says with a smile too wide. "We're here to help."

He leads me through the automatic doors, and I pause for a moment to take it in.

We step toward the automatic double doors, and they glide open as if expecting us. The lobby is a fairytale. Glass, light, marble, quiet luxury. I can almost hear my pulse echoing against the walls.

The lobby glows like a beacon, everything polished, everything gleaming. So bright and perfect. There's lobby music in the background that fills the air, like we're part of a movie set about glamour and fame.

"Wow," I whisper to myself.

My chest tightens slightly, though I can't tell if it's excitement or something else.

Scott looks at me and smiles as if he can sense my surprise. "Before we head upstairs, we'll need you to deposit your cell phone with Susan at the front desk."

I nod. Rules are rules. No phone. Josh was clear about this rule from the beginning. He mentioned Susan on our call. So far, so good.

As we shuffle to the front desk, Scott asks, "How was your flight?"

"Uneventful," I shrug.

"That's good to hear," he chuckles, his tone cheerful but just a touch off. Like a record skipping in the background.

Behind the desk stands a blonde woman with a wide, perfect smile. "Welcome! You must be Rachel, right?"

"That I am," I say.

"Wonderful. We'll be taking care of you for the next thirty days. Your stay is going to be easy, comfortable... pleasant." Her eyes glint too sharply behind the smile. "If you'll just hand me your phone, you can be on your way."

I give it to her without thinking. It feels strange handing over my lifeline, but I tell myself it's just part of the deal.

I turn to Scott, who's standing by my side and staring at me. Waiting. "Ready?"

Both he and Susan bore their eyes into me like I've missed something important. I haven't.

Scott says, "I'll take you upstairs now." He and Susan exchange a quick glance before he and I walk away.

Scott calls the elevator. We wait in silence, the soft hum of the lobby music filling the space.

"Have you been to Boston before?" he asks. Small talk—like he's trying to fill the space—but his eyes linger on me.

"No," I say. "I've heard good things, though."

From Roger. He bragged about the city a million times.

He nods quickly. "It really is a city of history. If you get a chance after your stay, take a tour. You won't regret it." He smiles. He's perfect for this role, whatever it is: a concierge?

Polite and unassuming. The kind of guy you'd call if you ever gotten into trouble.

The elevator arrives, doors sliding open with a whisper. Inside, soft music plays again. It's almost indulgent, decadent.

"I've heard why you're here," Scott says, voice lower now, almost confidential. "Lucky you. You couldn't have picked a better place."

"I didn't pick it," I reply. "It was chosen for me."

His eyebrows stitch together. "Hah. Strange."

I chuckle. "Strange? Why?"

He shrugs. "Oh, don't mind me. No reason."

I feel a flicker of unease, like he's hiding something just out of reach. My stomach twists, and I shift slightly, pretending to examine the floor numbers as the elevator crawls up.

We both watch the floor numbers inch by. The elevator moves agonizingly slowly, like it has nowhere to hurry to.

At last, the elevator slows and stops. The doors open. "Well, here we are. Twenty-first floor." Scott's voice is chirpy, like he's excited we're coming to an end of our interactions.

We step outside. The hallway is silent except for the faint hum of the air conditioning. Perfectly clean, perfectly still.

Scott stops at a door and pulls a card key from his pocket. I notice immediately: no room number.

"Uh... Scott? No room number?"

He quickly glances over his shoulder, then looks back at the door. "Ha. You're right. Honestly, I hadn't noticed before."

"Don't all hotel rooms have numbers?" I ask, voice rising just a notch. "How do the hotel staff identify it?"

"This is... special. Presidential Suite. Doesn't need a number." He gives a polite, slow smile. "Comforting?"

He turns around and works the door. Unlocks it.

I shrug, forcing a smile. "Sure. Totally."

The door swings open, and I notice a DO NOT DISTURB sign hanging around the knob, almost comically.

I halt sharply by the door, point at it. "Is that really necessary?" I ask, laughing lightly.

"That?" Scott points at it. "You'll see. Locked in for thirty days. But people do wander this floor when they shouldn't."

"Like who?" I ask, a shiver curling up my spine.

"Drunks," he says. "Tourists. Curious souls." His laugh echoes lightly down the hallway, just enough to unsettle me.

He sets my luggage on the floor and looks at me seriously. "Listen. The most important thing: we will take care of you. Rest now. Tomorrow, your journey begins."

"Right," I say. "What time is it now?"

I forgot to check before giving away my phone, and I don't have a watch.

Scott pulls his phone from his pocket. "It's almost ten."

Time flies—I hadn't realized it was so late. Plus, there's the three-hour difference between Vegas and Boston.

"Get some rest," Scott says.

I nod, but my stomach twists. Locked in. No phone. Thirty days. Everything feels so precise and orchestrated. But I force my legs to move, my thoughts to quiet.

Scott says goodbye, wishes me a good night sleep. Once the door clicks shut behind me, the suite unfolds like something from a dream—or a trap. Expansive, modern, immaculate. I run my hand along the edge of the fancy wood table, testing reality.

Thirty days. Thirty days to earn six million dollars.

I breathe in the scent of fresh linens, polished wood, and faint perfume lingering in the room. Gratitude washes over me, but a thread of unease weaves through it, thin and persistent.

I take a deep breath. *You've survived worse. You can do this.*

Somewhere in the quiet corners of the suite, a thought whispers back: *Or maybe you won't.*

I laugh softly, though it's hollow. Sleep comes quickly after that, but the quiet hum of the air conditioner feels less like comfort and more like a watchful eye.

I wake up in a haze of confusion, too disoriented to know where I am at first.

I just know I'm not in my depressing house that sucks the soul out of you.

Disorientation—it's bound to happen when the bed is harder than I am used to and the walls are brighter.

As far as I remember, at least according to Scott, I am in the Presidential Suite. On the twenty-first floor.

I lift my head from the pillow and look around. I study the room a little harder. Last night, I crashed as soon as I entered the room, so I didn't quite take the time to check out my new surroundings.

It looks different against the bright sunlight coming between the curtains covering the single large window.

The room takes my breath away. It isn't just a room. It's more like a small apartment—big, quiet. The bed is king-sized, the sheets smooth beneath my fingers, expensive in a way you feel immediately. Six hundred thread count, maybe. I don't need to check. It's the same kind Roger used to demand when we were married.

Six-hundred-thread count. Nothing less. He's always had high standards for these things. I learned them in the marriage—not before. It's funny how quickly you get used to luxury, how your brain recalibrates and starts to believe comfort is the default.

I laugh; the sound is quick and a little wrong in the silence.

I remove the sheets and remember that, when I arrived, there were silk pajamas waiting on my bed. That's what I'm wearing now. I dash to the enormous window and open the curtains only to be greeted by the stunning view of the Boston Common below.

"Wow."

I can't help but feel an amazing sense of happiness. How could anyone turn down this opportunity? How could anyone say no to this?

The Boston Common looks nearly deserted, but the sky is overcast, promising rain in the afternoon. That will keep me even more motivated to stay indoors and not feel guilty about it. At least not today. Vegas is sunny most of the time, the sunshine always beckoning me to go places, enjoy the day. But lately, I haven't done anything fun, because, let's be honest, I can't afford the lifestyle I used to have when Roger and I first married.

Before, it was brunch with the girls, then hitting up the spa and salon to have my nails done. Then a little shopping spree before I met Roger for dinner after work.

Roger's role in our marriage was to make our life secure and comfortable. Because I'd been unemployable for most of my adult life, my role stayed firmly within the marriage: to brighten his day when he came home, to make the darkness feel manageable. His older sister, Karen, used to call me a grifter. I understood her instinct to protect her brother. When acceptance failed, she resorted to badmouthing me, throwing stones if it made her feel better.

What she never understood was that Roger and I were codependent in our own way—until Roger realized I could no longer keep up my side of the bargain. That's when he decided his life might improve once we divorced.

I need to stop thinking about Roger for once.

I scan around the room and take a brief tour—in the room's corner is a round table with two chairs, and on the other side is a dresser with a mini fridge where a multitude of alcoholic drinks have been stored away: beer, vodka, whiskey, wine. On the bottom shelf, there are all kinds of soda and bottled water.

There's a vanity on the other side—large enough to store big items, but I won't need that.

The air smells of vanilla and lavender. I inhale the aroma

and close my eyes just for a second to take it all in. A happy feeling settles in my tummy, like that time I woke up looking at the vast Nevada desert and thinking the sky's the limit. And it's the small things that make life joyful.

I wander the room, taking everything in more carefully. The walls are white and sterile, more hospital than hotel. No paintings. No artwork at all. The emptiness unsettles me. Wouldn't a luxury hotel like this display something—anything—to soften the space, to make it feel lived in?

I've seen the photos of the luxury hotels. The rooms basking in wealth and beauty. And perhaps I am mistaken. Perhaps there are no paintings because I am not here to enjoy the beauty and wealth, after all.

That will happen if I survive this place.

"Shit," I murmur. "There's no TV here." I scoff. "What the fuck."

The absence of a TV is louder than anything. Where's the TV? I don't remember it being part of the rules—at least Josh didn't mention anything—but this realization hits hard.

Back at home, it was the only thing that broke the silence and made me feel less lonely. The only thing that anchored me in reality.

"Hmm, strange." I say to myself.

Now that I think more, I don't believe Josh said there would be no TV, but it could very well be in line with the rest of the rules: no contact from the outside world even if that implies seeing it on the screen.

I made a few circles around the room, as if the missing items would somehow appear. I stop by the dresser where I stored all my clothes—I only needed a couple of drawers. An envelope with my name across sitting on the top of the dresser gets my attention. It isn't sealed; I can tell right away, so I take and open it to find a folded piece of paper inside.

The note is typed out. Impersonal.

I've always enjoyed finding random notes around the house when I was married to Roger. He was romantic once, professing his love in haikus and short stories. Or just simply: have a nice day, darling.

But this here doesn't seem like a love note.

I read:

Dear Rachel,

Welcome to the adventure of your life!

I hope your stay is cozy and comfortable.

If you need anything, you won't be able to call us, since we have removed the phone from your room, but you could communicate to us using the camera in the far corner of the room.

I look up from the piece of paper. No hotel landline phone?

I didn't notice it was missing until I read the note. I'm

guessing they have a backup plan—probably a camera.

I scan the room, searching for it. My eyes dart along the edges of the ceiling until I spot it.

All right. It's there. And it feels like it's staring right at me.

I turn around as if trying to hide my face and continue to read:

We presume there are only two different times you might stand in front of the camera:

1) In case of emergency

2) You need something from the outside world.

In case of an emergency, the signal you use is standing still in front of the camera for exactly ten seconds, then walking away. Do not do this under any other circumstances. Emergency only.

For number two, when you need something from the outside world, use a hand gesture, like a wave, three times.

This camera is monitored 24/7, and someone will come to your room under either circumstance. The camera sees everything—even in the dark.

Meals will be delivered to your room three times a day: at 8 am, 1 pm, and 6 pm. No exceptions.

You can leave your room once a day, between 2

and 4 pm, but you are not allowed to leave the hotel premises.

Remember—it's only thirty days to complete this challenge.

We wish you the best of luck!

The Four Seasons Staff

"Hmm..." I murmur to myself. "The Four Seasons staff? How ominous."

These rules... they seem logical, but something is off about them. Whoever came up with them wanted to add another layer of challenge. Like being all alone in a room for thirty days isn't hard enough.

Besides, why is the letter from the Four Seasons staff, and not Josh? It's possible Josh was just a recruiter. Or just a guy coordinating the whole thing, and who knows, maybe the one who will be six million dollars lighter in thirty days.

Maybe all he cares about is that I've been delivered to the hotel.

It doesn't matter. I put the paper back on the dresser and walk to the corner to see the camera. There it is. Perched in the very corner of the ceiling, with a tiny red light blinking right at me.

I smile, wondering who's on the other side of the camera. Josh? I start to lift my arm, then stop myself. No gestures. No waving. That would mean I need something from the outside. I'm careful not to linger, not to stand there long enough to send the wrong signal. The rules are already engraved in my mind. Instead, I turn and walk away—though curiosity follows me.

There will be time to find out.

I stroll into the bathroom and gasp at the sight of it. Last night when I walked in, I don't remember it being this large. Oversized, it features an enormous tub, a double vanity, a Japanese toilet seat with heat and all, and a shower in the corner. There's a small closet on the other side of the room, and I open it to find a multitude of towels stacked up on every shelf. There's no shortage of them, that's for sure.

I run the water and sink into the tub once it's full. Ahh. I haven't relaxed like this in a long time. My small house in Vegas doesn't have a bathtub, and my spa days are long over.

The bathroom smells faintly of flowers—something sweet I can't quite place. I close my eyes and breathe it in. The water ripples with my movement, then stills. Warmth seeps into me, the quiet wrapping around my thoughts until it gently pulls me under.

I DON'T KNOW how much time has passed, but I hear the front door slam shut.

It jolts me awake.

The water by now is lukewarm, so I get out of the tub, shivering, and grab a towel from the closet. I wrap myself up and walk to the room to find a tray of food on the table—must be lunchtime.

The plate looks amazing: a small piece of blackened salmon, mashed potatoes, and a side salad. It looks delicious. My stomach growls. I skipped breakfast and slept through the morning, jet-lagged and exhausted from the flight. Or at least I assume I slept in. It doesn't feel like much time has passed between waking and this meal arriving at one o'clock.

Who brought it? Josh?

The primal urge wins. I am going to check if the door is unlocked even though I'm sure it isn't.

I glance at the camera, then cross to the door and twist the knob. Nothing. The door doesn't budge. Locked. I scoff. Of course, it's locked. I am not supposed to leave my room until somebody lets me out. The rules say once a day.

I shouldn't complain. It's totally manageable.

Now that I am thinking about leaving the room, I stop in my tracks. "Wait, what time is it?" I whisper to myself.

I sit down to eat my meal, and before I put the fork in my salmon, curiosity takes over me. I study the room's walls once again, only to be shocked by the discovery: I don't see a clock anywhere in the room. One is usually by the bed, on a side table, flashing at you, reminding you to get up and do things.

But there's none on either side of my bed.

Strange.

Maybe there's one hanging on the far wall; just a simple wall clock, ticking away, showing the time. Nothing fancy.

And let's face it—I don't need anything fancy. No alarms. No clocks to tell me AM or PM, or flip to military time if my heart desired. Where would I go anyway?

I just need something simple to orient myself, to help count the days to the finish line.

I've heard horror stories where people lose a sense of time—days blending into nights until they can't tell which way the clock hands are moving anymore. You question whether it's the clock that's wrong... or your mind. And you desperately try to get back on track... but fail.

I walk to the edge of the room and once again check every wall. Nothing.

Panic rises inside me, but I do my best to curtail it. I stop and take a deep breath.

After circling around the room, stumbling, wondering if it might be in front of my eyes, I simply can't see it. Exhaustion can do it to you—fresh places can do it to you—your eyes still catching up, your senses adapting to the new place.

You don't notice something missing—the small things we take for granted—until we crave them.

This can't be real.

I slide down the wall and stare at the door, stunned.

Dread completely consumes me when I realize: there is no clock anywhere in the room.

TEN
RACHEL BROWNING

A spell of dizziness consumes me; I hold on to the chair nearby so as not to fall.

What the hell?

No clock anywhere.

Not having a TV almost makes sense—almost—but not having a clock defies all logic. It has to be an oversight.

Is this part of the rule or game I missed somehow?

My mind is churning, thinking of the worst-case possibilities. What if all this is a farce, and they trap me here for longer than thirty days? Maybe I'll never leave. Maybe the luxury is just a lure, and the silence, the rules, the camera—they're all part of the cage.

A thought hits me harder than I admit.

For this arrangement here, there was nothing in writing. No binding contract. No waiver. Some assurance that I will be fine with whatever unfolds between these walls.

Josh was too zealous in ushering me to a place that apparently I could have chosen myself. Scott was a bit too surprised when I told him the hotel was chosen for me; maybe I did have a choice, and Josh said nothing.

Only a piece of paper that tells me when to wave and when to stand still.

I don't think of myself as naïve, but I was too desperate to make a deal and follow Josh's orders. No follow-up questions. Not even a single concern about what could go wrong. Only what he promised at the end.

I bet that's how they picked me: they smelled my desperation, my desire to get out of the hole.

I feel sick to my stomach.

A lot of this makes no sense.

I pace around the room, the food settling in my stomach. I feel sick. My heart hammers in my chest, and a dizzy spell takes over me.

It's the usual—my anxiety. This is something else entirely. When you know that time goes by, and you're indifferent to it. It feels like someone is trying to take complete control of me.

And I don't know what to do.

I suppose I could quit now. But quitting isn't an option when you think about that shitty house and no future prospects. I'm not a quitter, I keep telling that to myself.

I dash to the bed and lie down, facing the ceiling.

Desperate times call for desperate measurements, but I'll show them I'm better than that.

Think, think, think, damn it.

There's nothing to think about. Relax, Rachel. You're only on day one. And it's just a fucking clock. Get used to it.

Except...

How am I supposed to know when my meals are coming or when two o'clock rolls in, so that I can get ready for my two-hour freedom? Being here without being able to see what time it is seems wrong.

It has to be an oversight.

There's only one way to find out.

I step in front of the camera and stare at the red blinking light. I wonder again who's behind it, watching me. The two signals I can give out are now embedded in my mind: emergency or if I need something.

I need something for sure. Just a simple clock. Quick.

Aware that time is slipping—how much, I can't say—I lift my arm quickly, careful not to make it look urgent. When I was a kid, I used to call Mom for things that didn't really need her, until she finally told me to stop. Something about wolves. Oh, right—*don't be the girl who cried wolf.* Funny how that warning feels different now, when no one might hear me at all.

This is entirely different. I just need the answer.

As I rapidly wave my arm, three times, feeling self-conscious, I can only hope that the person watching me is on their way to my room. And that they saw me.

I trudge over to the table and sit down, rocking back and forth, my hands folded on my lap. And wait.

Time moves at the pace of molasses. The silence is heavy and suffocates.

Then a knock on the door.

It gets me excited. I put my hands on the tabletop and straighten myself.

Whoever is on the other side of the door is probably here to address my hand wave.

The door opens. They must have the key to my room. The idea unsettles me, though I feel a small, unexpected sense of relief. They are here. And that's all that matters.

A younger man—in his twenties—steps inside the room and closes the door behind. He's tall and skinny, dressed in pale blue from head to toe—the crisp suit with its striped trousers, the matching jacket, and a rounded pillbox hat that makes him look like he stepped out of an old black-and-white film.

He stares at me with his droopy eyes. His face is nondescript. I expect him to say something—anything—but he just keeps looking at me.

He looks off. By proximation, he's in his 20s, but he carries himself like an old man.

"Hi." I break the silence. "I called..."

"I know." He cuts me off; his words are razor sharp. "What is it you need?"

I tell him there's no clock in the room and ask if I can have one.

A lump rises in my throat. It feels ridiculous—asking for something so small, so ordinary—but I can't help it.

The man shrugs. "I'll ask and let you know." He heads to the door, but before he exits, he stops in his tracks and turns around. "I'll be back at two to let you out."

"Okay." I smile, feeling giddy. The room is pleasant, but I could use a change of scenery, get to know the hotel better. Before he exits, I call out after him. "Hey, what's your name?"

He turns around. "Alex."

Just as I'm about to say, "Nice to meet you," Alex is already out the door, slamming it shut.

That's when I first notice.

A deep, unsettling silence lingers in the room.

I press my palms against the edge of the bed and try to steady my racing thoughts.

There's a stark difference between Scott's and Alex's demeanor. Scott is overly pleasant, friendly, reassuring me that they're here to take care of me. Alex? He looks like someone roped him into this job as a punishment. I hope I don't have to deal with him for the whole thirty days.

I shake my head, get out of bed, and walk to the window to enjoy the view of the Boston Common. Alex should surely be back soon, but there's no sign of him—like he was never here.

***

IT HAS to be two pm when the door swings open again.

Between lunchtime and 2 p.m., the time stretched like an endless loop of events that made me feel trapped inside the same moment, over and over again. I keep thinking it's only day one, but if I find things to occupy my time with, I'm sure it will fly by.

Day one is almost over after all. There are only ten hours to go until day two. It's nothing compared to a lifetime of wealth.

Alex strolls through the door, looking at me with the same droopy eyes. "I asked about the clock. I was told we couldn't do that." He shrugs. His face remains unmoved, nondescript, like he couldn't care less. But I am reeling.

"What? Why?" I nearly squeal.

He shrugs again. "Beats me. I do as I'm told. They don't tell me anything." He looks up at his wristwatch and says, "You can leave your room... now. You have two hours to walk around the premises, but you can't leave the hotel."

I nod. "I know."

"Good."

He turns around to walk to the door and lets me know when I ask him, in a low voice. "Do you think I can borrow your watch?" I'm making the face you make when you instantly realize asking that question was a bad idea.

Alex stares at me and says, "No, I can't do that." He gives his watch a quick glance and looks up. "It's a gift from my father. Besides, they already said no."

Defeat washes over me. "Who's *they*?"

He's quiet for a moment, then says. "The people who brought you here."

"You mean... Josh?"

He shrugs. "I don't know their names, okay? And stop asking me questions."

Alex drags a hand down his face, lips pressed thin, like he's counting the seconds until this is over. He stands by the door waiting for me to get moving. I do. I walk through the door slowly, like they are sending me to a firing squad.

This is the first time I've seen the walls outside my room since arriving, and the hallway comes into sharp focus.

It isn't how I remember it. Or maybe I never really saw it at all—maybe it was too dark that first night, and I missed the patterns and colors closing in around me.

The wallpaper is white and lightly textured, the tiny bumps catching beneath my fingertips. The carpet is a clean, unsettling blue, patterned with shapes that almost—but not quite—resemble flowers.

It feels wrong. Like something out of an old, abandoned building, not a luxury hotel.

I shudder.

Alex strides in front of me. I follow him like a helpless child.

"Where are we going?" I ask when we reach the door at the end of the hall.

"Wherever you want." He says, then opens the door and disappears. The thud of Alex's steps reverberates through the stairway as he descends.

Now, I stand there alone, where he left me, wondering if I should simply follow him or wait until enough distance has formed between us. I wait.

As I look around, something unsettles me.

I don't see any other doors on the floor. No numbered rooms. No subtle signs of life. Just me.

The walls on either side are bare, stretching on longer than they should, uninterrupted and silent. I tell myself this must be intentional—that the Presidential Suite is designed this way, tucked away for guests who pay for isolation as much as luxury. Extreme privacy. Extreme quiet.

That explanation settles briefly in my stomach. Didn't Scott hint at how isolated the hotel wants to keep the floor from people who stumble on it?

The doubt doesn't disappear. It shifts. Grows heavier as I picture myself alone on an entire floor, sealed off from the rest of the hotel.

It's fine, I tell myself. If something happens, there's always the camera. Someone would see. Someone would come.

Still, the thought doesn't comfort me the way it should.

I push open the exit door Alex walked through seconds ago and step into the stairwell. The door closes behind me with a final, echoing thud. As I descend, my nerves hum beneath my skin, each step taking me farther from the suite and deeper into parts of the hotel I haven't seen yet.

I don't have a plan. I just keep moving.

It will be good to find other people, I tell myself. Hear other voices. A sign of normalcy. Maybe a clock—something solid and measurable—will make this place feel less strange.

Less like it's watching me move through it.

ELEVEN

RACHEL BROWNING

If my room feels silent, the rest of the hotel is just as eerily quiet. Only that same lobby music blooming in the background, as I get closer to life.

It's not what I expect to see when I arrive at the main lobby.

It's pretty strange to see there are no people in the lobby, not something I'd expect to see in an upscale hotel.

Back home, I'm used to loud spaces. Even at home, when Roger and I first married, we had music playing in the background, and when we moved to the new house, when things weren't as happy anymore, the TV was on almost all the time. It didn't matter what was on: news, commercial, shows —we watched it all to distract ourselves from the claustrophobia.

Noise meant life.

The lobby is vast and immaculate, the type of space

designed to impress, yet it feels oddly depressing today. Polished marble floors gleam beneath towering chandeliers, but the light they cast is cold, almost clinical, leaving shadows where there shouldn't be any. Plush velvet chairs sit in careful clusters, perfectly aligned, untouched—I can see specks of dust on the headrests—as if waiting for guests who never arrive. The front desk stretches wide and unoccupied, its brass accents dulled by the silence. Even the air feels staged—kind of still and stuffy—and as I stand there, I get the unmistakable sense that the lobby isn't meant to comfort me.

It's meant to observe.

I must be tripping, but it looks so different from how I remember it when I first saw it last night. As far as I remember, there was a large mural on the wall behind the front desk, and the desk itself was decorated with gigantic bouquets of fresh flowers you simply couldn't miss.

Perhaps my memory is playing games with my mind.

I look up at the ceiling to check if the lobby is adorned with surveillance cameras like my room is—every corner has one, staring at me, daring me to move.

I do.

I come closer to the front desk and face the front sliding door. I stop in my tracks and stare at it—the moving cars on the street, an occasional passerby, the glimpse of the Boston Common—they all beckon me to the outside.

"Can I help you?" the deep voice behind the desk startles me.

I turn around and see a rigid-looking, tall man standing behind the desk, shooting daggers at me.

"I'm just observing." I say like I'm making an excuse for being here. "I'm staying at the…"

"I know who you are." The man cuts me off. "You're staying in the Presidential Suite on the twenty-first floor."

A creepy smile flickers across his face, gone almost before I can place it. His bloodshot eyes don't blink, fixed and glassy, and for a moment he looks less like a man than a damaged statue—something cracked, propped upright, and barely pretending to be alive. Frankenstein comes to mind.

The first thought that occurs to me is that neither Scott nor Susan is around. It's quite possible that it's not their shift now, or they could have a day off today, but this man's demeanor demands answers. Just like Alex's. It's strikingly different from how I was greeted yesterday.

I approach the front desk reluctantly and ask for Susan.

His bloodshot eyes fix on me. His mouth opens only slightly. "There's no Susan here."

I tilt my head. "That can't be right." A small laugh slips out. "She checked me in yesterday." He doesn't react. Just keeps staring. "She took my phone."

"Are you sure?" he asks, his voice flat, cold.

I don't give him time to push further. I smile instead and change course. "What do you suggest I do at the hotel for the next two hours?"

He lifts an arm and points to his left, his eyes never

leaving mine. The gesture feels wrong—unnatural. "There's a spa over there. And a swimming pool," he says. "If you need an outfit, someone will assist you."

"Great." I smile and head in the direction he indicated. His eyes follow me the entire time, tracking my movement as if he's making sure I don't veer off course. I have no intention of escaping. Not yet.

Just before I turn the corner, I glance back. "The hotel's awfully quiet," I say. "Where is everybody?"

He stares at me. "I don't know."

His voice is even-keeled and robotic, like he's been drugged and running on autopilot. I consider asking his name, but the thought makes my stomach tighten. Some questions feel dangerous here—and I'm not ready to find out which ones cross the line.

I shrug, "Alrighty then."

I feel his eyes bore into my back as I walk away from him. Does he think I want to escape?

I walk to the spa, but a funny feeling sits in the pit of my stomach. I don't see a single person in sight. The space is deserted, like we're in the apocalypse aftermath.

At least the spa looks like an oasis in the middle of a desert. Stunning. Every surface gleams, every detail carefully curated. For a moment, relief washes over me. I could spend my time here. I could make this work.

I let out a small laugh. A swimming pool sits at the center of the room, steam rising softly from the water. Along the wall, several individual saunas stand in a neat row. This, I think, is how I'll survive the next twenty-nine days. I've missed this kind of pampering—the slow afternoons, the laughter with friends that once filled spaces like this.

I walk over to the saunas and pull on the first door. It doesn't budge.

"What the heck?"

I try the next one. Locked. The next. Still locked. All of them are sealed shut, pristine and useless.

"Strange," I murmur.

Luxury hotels have schedules, closures, maintenance windows. That must be it. I must have caught it at a bad time.

The explanation feels thin—but for now, it's the one I choose to believe.

I park myself in a pool chair by the window and glance at the swimming pool; the water is clean; the pool well maintained—it looks inviting enough for me to consider going for a swim.

I swirl in the chair and look through the window, a lonely building sitting across the street. It's just a simple structure—plain walls and windows stacked up in rows and columns. Boston is an old city—it's no surprise the buildings here sit on top of each other.

I simmer in silence, weighing my options. I could stay here and wait for someone—Alex, maybe—to escort me back to my room. Or I could swim a few laps, burning off the restless energy coiling inside me.

Either way, there isn't much to do.

The man at the front desk said someone would help me with an outfit, but the spa is empty. A little too empty. "Hello?" I call, my voice echoing faintly off the tiled walls. No answer.

Either he wasn't telling the truth... or something else is going on.

I pace the space, listening to the soft lap of water against the pool's edge and the distant blare of car horns drifting in from the street. For the first time since I arrived, I feel a sharp, unexpected ache for human contact. Where is everyone when you actually need them?

It's a strange thing. When you're alone by choice, solitude feels like freedom. You can seek company or avoid it whenever you want. But when that choice is taken away, the desire for connection multiplies. What we can't have is always what we want most.

Roger would be laughing at me if he knew what I'm up to. He always thought I couldn't survive being alone for long periods of time. Shit. He could be right.

Right now, I'd welcome anyone. Anyone at all. Even the creepy guy at the front desk. Maybe I could talk to him, try to make conversation, even though he didn't seem willing— or capable.

Still, it's worth a try.

I stand and head straight for the door, twisting the knob without hesitation. I freeze. Locked. I tug again, harder this time. Nothing. The door doesn't move.

This has to be a mistake. It's only mid-afternoon. Why would hotel staff lock the door to the poolroom?

Did I lock it on my way in? Did the man at the front desk lock it to ensure I don't escape?

Makes no sense.

I'm not going anywhere.

I pound my fist against the door, calling for help. "Anybody there? Open the door!"

I latch onto the doorknob and twist it like my life depends on it. I call again. The door is so heavy and thick, I highly doubt anyone can hear me. Even after many attempts, no one is coming to my rescue, and I am feeling trapped here.

I don't even know how much time has lapsed, but I give up.

I walk back to the closest chair and slide down, observing the outside. It's started to rain, and the sky has turned gray and cloudy. Then, thunder and lightning roll in, opening up the sky like it's going to swallow the world. Boston has more humid days; not a surprise.

The thunder is a massive crash of noise. That's probably the reason I didn't hear the door open.

Someone taps me on the shoulder. I scream. When I turn around, I see Alex, with his droopy eyes, looking at me while standing still like a soldier. "It's time to go back to your room."

"Is it already four o'clock?" I ask, somewhat surprised and relieved. Maybe time does move fast.

He simply nods.

I stand up and follow him. He opens the door with ease. Unlocked now, but it wasn't just minutes ago.

I ask him, incredulously. "Alex... can you tell me why the door was locked while I was in here?"

"Which door?"

"The door that leads to the swimming pool. I tried to get out, but the door was locked."

He stops for a second, then glances at me over his shoulder. "Locked?" He scoffs. "I don't think so."

Heat rushes to my face. The dismissal lands harder than I expect, like I've imagined the whole thing. "What? Yes, it was locked. I tried to open the door so many times—I'm sure it was locked."

"The hotel never locks the door during the operation hours."

"What are the operation hours?"

"Seven A.M. to ten P.M."

"I don't get it," I insist. "Are you sure the door never locks?"

He scoffs and rolls his eyes in annoyance. He doesn't even answer my question.

We stride through the lobby and get to the elevators.

Alex pushes the UP button and gazes at me. "Maybe you're just not strong enough to open the door."

My jaw drops. I bite back a response. I'm not a body-builder, but I'm not fragile either.

The elevator door dings upon arrival, and we step inside. When I turn around, I see the front desk man boring his eyes at me, giving me a lopsided smile. Between him and Alex, and the locked door, it feels like I'm in the *Twilight Zone*. But I can't go down that rabbit hole. I have to stay positive if I want to survive.

The elevator doors close, and we rise. Alex stares at a single point on the ceiling, unmoving. I want to speak, to break the quiet, but the words die in my throat.

When we get to the floor, he rushes to my room—the only room on the floor—and opens the door wide. "Here. I'll see you tomorrow."

I trudge through the door, every step heavy, like some-one's been beating me senseless all day. Sitting alone in silence suddenly doesn't feel so appealing. But I remind myself: I've survived worse. Thirty days alone can't be that bad.

The day is almost over.

And there are only twenty-nine days left.

Then it hits me—Alex's words echo in my mind: *See you tomorrow*. What did he mean? Shouldn't he drop off my dinner at six?

No more fancy clothes and expensive trips.

Geez, Roger. You couldn't soften the blow at least a bit?

He drops the news like it's a hot potato he's been dying to toss. I get his concern: his business is going to shit, and he's on the verge of bankruptcy. So much for the royal treatment —this train just pulled into the last station.

Roger was generous. I can't even count the number of times he bought me things I never asked for, or whisked me away on trips I didn't really need. Back then, it felt flattering... indulgent... almost magical.

And now this. No more.

He means it. It stinks more than I'm willing to admit.

But I feel he's hiding something. Sure, AI can be partially to blame, but there's no way his business will crumble in a heartbeat, because everyone suddenly uses a robot to design their interior.

There has to be something deeper, more troublesome.

Must have something to do with William.

I remember now Roger complaining about how William had these "crazy ideas" that he wanted Roger to implement. They didn't see eye to eye, and Roger was making plans to kick William out of their business. Surely, William wouldn't mind. He's already aged, ripe for retirement, and not as sharp as he used to be.

But William did mind. He wanted to be part of it until the bitter end, making decisions for the company. He might have been ready for retirement, but his sharp mind wasn't willing to give in yet.

I can't think of a better reason William is now dead—Roger hates the fact William disagreed with him.

Roger couldn't convince him to sell half of his business. The way he talked to him on the landing—with such intensity, rage, resolve—only means Roger was getting frustrated because he wasn't succeeding. And what did he do?

Pushed him to his death.

I take my Diet Coke and swivel it around before I take a sip. "Okay." But deep inside, I'm reeling. "We don't need to take extravagant trips anymore. That's fine."

"The worst part..." Roger chokes a bit. "The worst part is that if the business does poorly, I don't know what's going to happen in the long run."

I take a pause. What does he mean exactly? Does he mean us?

"Look," I lift my right palm facing him, "I'm no expert, but I don't believe for a second AI will ruin your business. I get your point, but there's nothing like the human touch to make things great. Right?"

Roger shakes his head. "You don't understand. People don't care about perfection anymore. It's all about money. If they want to cut corners, they'll find a way and convince themselves it's good enough. AI already does the job."

"What about hotels? Do you think they would replace humans with AI?" I sound incredulous. Life doesn't turn around and slap you with its tail on its way out. It doesn't work like that. But Roger doesn't want to hear my reassurances.

"I appreciate you saying all this, but I'm already feeling the dent in my checking account."

We stare at each other.

"Listen, you already said no more trips. I'm okay with that."

This begs repetition, but I hate the sound of it. I'm definitely going to miss my luxury items, Gucci bags and Prada shoes, last-minute trips, the promises... but something deep inside tells me this is not his biggest concern.

Roger now looks like a kid whose candy was taken away. Too tired. His face is wrinkly. Jesus, he's only thirty-nine. Looks a bit too old for his age.

Let's be honest, sex hasn't been that great either. Lately, it's been a more mechanical type of activity; no emotions, no excitement, nothing really that wants me to keep wanting more, coming back for it.

Can't blame AI for that one!

This could be the beginning of the end of us.

Now William's murder. The one he's hiding from me, because surely, he should have told me by now. This one hit hard.

I can't trust Roger with the same intensity anymore.

He keeps gazing at his phone as if it's a lifeline. The waitress finally brings our food—a bowl of pasta for Roger and a salad for me—and something shifts.

We don't speak while we're eating our meals.

It's like we know, we feel this is the end.

One thing Roger doesn't know is that after this dinner, I can go to the cops and tell them what I saw earlier tonight. I can tell Roger what I saw and use it for blackmail. Or, I can let it go and pretend I didn't see anything and let karma decide his fate.

Nah, the third option isn't an option.

Maybe Roger will tell me after eating his bowl of pasta. Have another drink. He must be rattled with nerves and fear, and he's probably finding the opportune moment to say something. He could have said something in the car, but it was too sudden. Murder still fresh on his hands.

And let's face it, a restaurant isn't the best place to confess murder.

But maybe he won't say he murdered William tonight. Or tomorrow. Maybe he won't even say that William is dead.

He's busy twirling pasta on his fork and shoving it into his mouth. He doesn't even look at me.

The waitress comes by, and Roger orders another double martini, as if two aren't enough. Roger likes to drink, but not like this. He's a moderate drinker, the type that likes to have a good laugh and have fun.

But Roger hasn't laughed once the entire evening. Not even cracked one genuine smile.

And why would he?

Roger has a lot to consider. His crumbling business, declining clientele, uncertain future.... I wouldn't smile if I were him.

And worst of all—Roger has murder on his hands.

I wake up from a nightmare, somewhat dazed and unsure of where I am.

It's an inevitable state here, which means I haven't quite accepted this room as my new abode.

It's still nighttime, darkness enveloping the room.

I sit up in bed and look through the window, faint lights projecting from the nearby building, a faint sporadic hum of traffic below. There's no way to find out what time it is, but judging by the darkness and some noise, it has to be at least close to dawn.

I swing my legs to the side and get up. On my way to the bathroom, I notice something sitting on the floor next to the entrance door. There's a slight movement, like something gentle is being released into the air.

I turn on the lights and see a tray of food—breakfast. A single croissant, a small dish with a variety of fruit, butter and jelly and a jug of coffee... steam is coming out of the jug, now realizing what the movement was. The coffee is hot. Too hot to realize that the tray had to have been delivered just recently.

I shake my head. "Wait a second. Is it already eight in the morning?"

I instinctively run to the window and open the curtains only to be greeted by the vast view of the Boston Common, still lit by the light poles. It's still very much dark outside. A few cars are passing by; I can see the silhouette of a single person walking across the Common; but it's otherwise empty.

Something seems wrong.

Maybe I keep forgetting the breakfast delivery time. I could swear the rules said eight a.m., but maybe my mind is playing tricks on me. I've never been good at memorizing numbers anyway. I can't even remember the exact date my mom died—trauma has a way of erasing things like that. But this is different. This is just a breakfast delivery time. Easy enough to remember.

I run to the dresser and grab the piece of paper with the welcome note. My eyes dart all over the paper until I find the bit stating the food delivery times.

Breakfast is at 8 am.

I was right. 8 o'clock.

"Damn it." I hate it when I doubt myself.

Of course, without the clock or any indicator of time, I

second-guess myself. But shit—who says it's not eight? Maybe the darkness in Boston doesn't lift until later in the morning. But wait—we're not in Sweden, for Christ's sakes. I had never been to Boston, but I know enough that the sun rises around the same time as it does in Vegas. They're on a similar latitude. Yes? No? Maybe. I've never been good at geography.

Regardless, there's no way it's eight right now.

And if I am right, and all the bets are I am, why wasn't the tray delivered on time? Are they breaking their own rules?

I didn't hear the door open. Everything feels off, and I wish I'd caught whoever snuck into my room. I've been sleeping like a log for the past two nights. Sleep has been my closest ally since I arrived—offering a small comfort when the loneliness creeps in.

The food can't go to waste. I pick up the tray and put it on the nearby table, then go to the bathroom. Silence is deafening. Heavy.

I have this funny feeling in the pit of my stomach that someone's fucking with me. Is it Josh? The guy at the front desk? Alex? Maybe not Alex. He's just a guy who gets orders and executes them.

Maybe I'm imagining it all. Jet lag and new places can get you out of sorts. But I know I'm not mistaken—it is not past eight o'clock yet.

It's all confusing. All of it. But there has to be an explanation.

I meander to the corner of the room and stand in front of the camera. The red light is flashing. It never quits. I wave my hand once, twice, three times, and step away. I walk back to the bed and lie down, staring at the ceiling, waiting for Alex to show up.

The sky outside is looking brighter, like the sun is trying to creep up the sky and wake up the city. As far as I know, in August, the sun rises around six in the morning, reassuring me that the breakfast delivery has to be a mistake.

The door opens. Alex walks in. He makes just a few steps forward until he stops in the smack middle of the room.

"Yes?" he says.

I smile, but my anxiety makes everything about me fake, including my smile. "I was... I was just wondering what the breakfast tray is doing here so early."

He scrunches his face. "What do you mean?"

"According to the rules, it's supposed to be here at eight, and I don't think it's even seven yet."

Alex says nothing. Just stands there and stares at me, making for a long, awkward silence.

"Say something, for Christ's sake!" I lose my cool for a moment.

He keeps staring, squints his eyes.

"You don't understand." I continue. "When you don't have a clock or watch, and someone brings you food outside the rules, it can drive you crazy." My voice sounds alarming. Desperate.

"No. I get it," Alex finally says. He's casual, like this is no big deal. But it is. And I need to know what is happening. "It's not me who brought it up. I can ask, but I don't know if I'm going to get any answers."

Why? Why wouldn't he get any answers?

I nod. "Okay. Thank you, Alex. I appreciate it."

Alex gazes at the camera for a second, then turns toward me. "Anything else?"

I'm desperately trying to keep him a little longer, ask questions, even if he has no answers to them, but my mind is drawing a blank. Definitely on overdrive with anxiety. I shake my head, but I hope to God things will get easier.

My heart is pounding so hard it feels wrong, each beat loud and erratic, and then it hits me—with a sickening jolt—I never packed my anxiety meds. I didn't even think about them. With only two hours to get ready, they never crossed my mind.

The realization settles in my chest, heavy and suffocating. I try to breathe through it, counting the inhales the way my therapist taught me, but the air feels thin, uncooperative. This place, this silence, presses in on me, and without the medication, I have nothing to dull the edge.

I tell myself it's fine. I've managed before. I can manage now.

But my body doesn't believe me.

Maybe it's not this place messing with my mind. It has to be me.

"Okay. Well, the next meal comes at one, and you're free to walk around the hotel at two. See you then."

With that, Alex turns around and walks through the door. The steam from the coffee has dwindled. I should probably eat and get some energy for the day, but my stomach is tied in knots. Instead of grabbing the pastry, I bolt for the bathroom, kneel to the floor, and retch.

I wipe my mouth with my hand, prop myself up, and hang over the sink.

"Ugh." I blurt. "What the fuck!"

I splash my face with cold water, as if it's going to help manage my anxiety. The thought of not having my meds is scary enough—like placing a cherry on top of a disgusting-looking cake.

I crawl back to the bedroom.

The sun is finally up. A full day looms ahead of me—and I already don't trust it.

The traffic below hums; low, muffled voices emerge. Boston is a busy city—not New York City-type busy—but you can definitely differentiate between day and night. There's no mistake the city is coming alive, everyone rushing to their destination while I'm here, in the presidential suite.

Waiting.

That's what it is. A waiting game. Waiting for my meals, waiting to be let out for a couple of hours, waiting for Day 30, waiting for a better life to come. Waiting strips meaning from time until every minute feels the same, and the room begins to feel less temporary and more like a sentence. Waiting is acceptable when we choose it, and I guess I have. But it's still fucking hard.

I'm lying in bed, watching the sky brighten with the sunrays. If I'm to guess what time it is, I would think it's about seven in the morning. No proof, it just feels like it.

Day two at the hotel.

I won't lie—things have been a little discouraging around here. Between no clock or watch to see the time go by and questionable people I've encountered at the hotel so far—like the man at the front desk and Alex—I'm growing concerned that things are not as organized or going as I expected them to.

But there has to be a good reason, right?

Josh warned me I was going to be their first one and to "bear with them," so I need to give him the benefit of the doubt. So what if the food got dropped at six, not eight? The dinner was delivered promptly last night. No complaints.

In the larger scheme of things, it's not a big deal. As long as I get the food... beggars can't be choosers. At least, that's what I tell myself.

As I lie in bed, my thoughts run to Roger. I can't help it. Mind does its own thing in solitude. Memories of our first meeting, our marriage, and our divorce flash through my mind.

It was three years ago that I first laid eyes on Roger. He was rolling a die at the casino, his biceps flexing with the motion. He caught my gaze from across the floor, and I waved at him innocently. He smiled back, and I drifted toward his table slowly. I liked his focus, his determination as he played—every so often, he'd glance at me and smile.

Free drinks circulated across the floor. A waitress stopped at our table, and he took two—one for him, one for me. Martinis. I remember it like it was yesterday. Those martinis, strong as hell. The first sip burned all the way down. I'm not much of a drinker, but I don't mind one or two on occasion.

That evening, we went to the club at the Palms Casino Resort, the music so loud it vibrated through my body. We danced all night, and sometime after the third drink, we ended up in his room—how we got there, I still can't remember.

The distant sound from the outside somehow shifts my thoughts.

Music.

I have always loved music. The kind you dance to all night, like Roger and I did the first night we met.

Music.

Roger used to dabble on his guitar some nights, like he was serenading me, and even though it was all a big joke, that's when I truly fell in love with him. The way he looked at me, like there was nothing and no one in the world but me.

That's when it hits me.

My stay here could be a lot more fun if I had music blasting. I'd feel less alone... less lonely. As much as I hate stepping in front of that camera and waving again, there's nothing in the rules about a daily limit. If I needed something, that's what it was there for. Available whenever I decided I needed it. And right now, I need music.

I swing my legs off the bed and stand, making a beeline for the corner where the camera blinks tirelessly. Thank God it's well hidden—the red light isn't noticeable until you're close. If it flashed constantly, out in the open, it would drive me insane. I'm half-way there already.

Somewhat hesitantly, I pull my robe more tightly and wave at the camera. Alex was here recently, so I'm afraid of leaving the impression of being needy. But how else would I communicate?

I'm overthinking. I need to stop.

I smile in the hope that it changes anything and step aside. Silence once again becomes heavy, and I realize the music would spice things up around here.

I trot over to the table and grab the pastry, taking a bite. The coffee has become cold by now, but I take a sip and swish it around my mouth. Tastes different being cold, but at least it helps perk me up.

In exactly twenty-eight days, I'll be able to afford a trip to the Maldives—a place I've always wanted to visit—watching the ocean beneath my feet from a house perched on the water. Just thinking about it makes me relax.

I finish the pastry and drain my coffee, but Alex is a no-show. In the past, he appeared relatively quickly—what felt like minutes later. This time, it's as if he's dragging his feet. Maybe I'm right. Maybe I do seem excessively needy. But they must understand what it's like to be locked in a room with nothing to do but stare at bare walls.

I go back to bed and lie down, glancing at the door now and then. Still no Alex.

Impatience begins to grate on me.

What if something happened to him? Did he quit? It wouldn't surprise me, not with how unhappy he looked. I stand and drift to the window when a thought occurs to me. To break the silence, I could open it—let in the hum of traffic, the distant voices from the street below. Breathe in fresh air. Oh gosh, yes—fresh air.

The window is large, rectangular, the one that stretches from the floor to the ceiling. There's a lever to pull on the side, but when I try, nothing happens.

"Fucking window."

I yank at it again, desperate to open it, but neither the window nor the lever will budge.

"Damn it."

Maybe I'm just not strong enough to pull it open.

I huff and puff, taking a break before I try again. Then the voice—

"What are you doing?"

I whirl to see Alex standing by the closed door. I didn't hear him come in.

"Nothing." I feel my heart in my throat, pounding like a drum.

He takes one step closer. "Doesn't look like it's nothing." He tilts his head. "Are you trying to open the window?"

Alex's voice is even keeled, like it always is. But he looks different this time, strangely enough, since I saw him once already this morning.

"Yeah, is that okay?" I'm trying to sound as casual as possible, but my voice sounds wobbly, uncertain.

Alex shakes his head. "I don't advise that you do." He takes another step forward.

"Why?"

In the back of my mind, I've already decided to open the window—make it happen—just to hear the cars passing and birds chirping.

"Because..." Alex scoffs. "Because there's an enormous drop to the street, and if you fall, you will be dead."

I flinch. "I... just want fresh air, that's all."

Here I am, reduced to a small child begging for candy, and Alex is the sort of parent who ignores the pleading.

"Now, what do you need this time?"

I almost forgot.

"I was wondering if I could have music in the room. It would be nice to kill the silence, you know..." I chuckle.

Alex shakes his head while boring his eyes on me. "No. Sorry."

My heart sinks. "Oh, shouldn't you check first?" I plead with him even though Alex has already delivered the verdict.

"I'm pretty sure they won't allow it." *They* again. Who's *they*? "Is that it? Anything else I can do for you... while I'm here?"

I am not ready to let Alex go just yet. "Yes. I have one more question."

We let the silence settle in, building awkward tension in the room.

"What is it?" Alex raises his voice, but his eyes are still, calm.

"Why was the breakfast delivered earlier than eight?"

"I don't know." He shrugs. "It must have been an oversight."

I do my best to stay calm, but inside, I feel like a thousand ants are crawling up my spine.

"What do you mean? Don't you have a watch?"

He puts his arm up to look at the watch, stares at it for a few seconds, then puts the arm down.

"I don't," he says.

"What? You don't?"

He looked at it seconds ago.

This is how trust erodes. You lean on someone, count on them to deliver on their promises, rules... and they can't deliver.

He looks up and gives me a small smile. "I can't. My watch stopped working last night at midnight."

The silence across the table is suffocating. Especially since Roger won't even look at me. His eyebrows have been stitched together since we arrived. He looks pensive, as if something has been gnawing at him—I can only imagine why. But he still hasn't said anything yet.

Suddenly, Roger looks up from his bowl of pasta, wipes his mouth and says, "You've been watching me all night like I did something wrong."

I flinch. "What?"

It's not every day you witness a murder and try to hide knowing it. To be honest, I'm seeing Roger in a brand-new light. A man whose business is collapsing, a man who no longer wants to care for me, a man who murders his partner and does nothing about it.

"Yeah. The look on your face," he continues. "I know you're disappointed that I can't afford things anymore, but you seemed reserved the second we set foot in this place. Like you're hiding something. What is it?"

I shake my head. "Nothing. It's nothing."

I put the straw in my mouth and take a sip of my diluted soda.

"Come on, Felecia. I know you well by now. You look like you've seen a ghost. And you're not talking much. You like to talk a lot."

Look who is projecting.

I wave my hand at nothing. Put my head down to avert his gaze. "It's just a headache."

Besides, fuck you, Roger. If you don't want to say anything, why should I?

"I swear I've never seen you like this before." Roger is insistent.

I curl my lip. "Listen, everything's fine. Although I must admit I'm a little shaken by what's happening with your business. I never thought, you know..." my words trail off.

I still feel he's lying to me. Like he could be lying that his car is in the shop, with brakes busted.

He shrugs. "Times are tough. Technology's evolved. But things will be fine."

Fine. I wonder how fine. People say that just to make themselves feel better even when it means shit.

"I gotta use the bathroom." He gets up abruptly and walks away from the table.

I sit there, stirring my Diet Coke, thinking about everything he said. About the business, about AI, about the trouble he might be having. I can't help but feel this strange mix of sympathy and unease. Part of me wants to console him, to say that his talent can't just be replaced by technology, but another part wonders how much of this is just his own fear talking. Or, how much of it is the truth.

If William is no longer alive, I'm sure his business will crumble even more.

Minutes later, I do a double take when I see Roger standing outside, holding his phone in his hand. He's not talking.

He's just outside the window, his hand placed on his forehead, like he's just listening. If I can judge by his demeanor, he seems distressed, worried about something. I wonder what message he's listening to. He looks over in my direction. Fear in his eyes.

He hangs up and walks back into the restaurant. He slides into his seat, his face a couple of shades lighter.

He looks to his right, then at me with those scary eyes and leans forward. "We need to talk."

No time.

No music.

No TV.

Nothing to keep me distracted in the room.

Not a single friendly face. No one to make this stay even tolerable.

For the first time, being here feels like a trap.

It's only day two, and I'm already craving the outside world. The sounds. The smells. People. Hell, I'd even take rude ones just to feel alive again.

I pace back and forth around my room.

What did Josh say when we talked over the phone the other day? I could bring books only. If my memory serves me right, he said I could bring five. Magazines and crossword puzzles. I don't have any of it here. Only a single pen, and nothing to write on.

The only problem is I'm not much of a reader, so how do I pick the genre, the author?

I can only hope one p.m. is rolling around soon. Alex will drop off a tray with my lunch, and I can ask him.

I wonder if he's tiring of me, asking all these questions, demanding things. He's just a messenger with a pillbox hat and not in a position to decide or change the terms of my stay.

I plod over to the bathroom to brush my teeth and stop in front of the gigantic mirror at the sink. I do a double take when I notice my saggy face. Oh, Jesus. It's not just the lack of makeup. It's like something is eating away at me—slowly hollowing me out from the inside, tugging at my skin, draining the color from my cheeks. I look older than I did yesterday. Maybe even older than I did last night.

"I look like shit," I whisper to myself.

Luckily, I brought my makeup bag with me. Even if I don't go outside or socialize, I still want to look good for myself. Human. I retrieve the bag and go back to the bathroom, pulling out the mascara and the eyeliner.

Roger used to call me a doll face when I put on too much makeup, and over the years, he conditioned me to tone it down a little, choose the shades that don't scream too much. In retrospect, it was his way of saying he didn't want me to draw attention.

Roger was extremely jealous. He'd do anything to shield me from other men's hungry eyes.

I put on my eyeliner, immediately make a giant booboo, and smear it halfway up my eyelid, instantly transforming myself into some warrior guy from the Amazon.

"Shit!"

Am I out of practice already?

I hear the door open and close, and I run back to the room.

Alex is standing in the middle of the room, holding a tray of food. Lunchtime.

Since breakfast, the time stretched painfully slowly.

And Alex? For a strange reason, I am happy to see him again.

He widens his eyes and retrieves, "What happened to you?"

I look at the eyeliner in my hand. "Oh, this?" I wave my hand, "it's nothing, don't worry."

He dashes to the table and places the tray on top. "Hope you enjoy your meal."

For the first time since I met him, he sounds more normal, human—not speaking in his robotic voice I'm used to for the last couple of days. Maybe he's just nervous, tending to me like a prisoner, and I don't blame him. I would feel like I'm doing someone's dirty job if I were he.

"Thank you." I smile.

"I'll let you out soon, okay? Then you can go for a little walk."

I cock my head. "That sounds wonderful, Alex." He gives a quick nod. "And how's your day been?"

Truthfully, I'm doing anything I can to keep him around a little longer—before I completely become a victim of my anxiety and lose my mind. Maybe I can even get some information out of him, like who he goes to when he needs to double-check the rules. Not that it would change anything. Still, there's something about being in the know that makes the world feel a little lighter.

He shrugs. "Not bad."

"Does it get busy around here?" I chuckle.

He keeps avoiding my gaze, and I wonder if it has anything to do with the liner smeared on my face.

"So-so," he says. "I mean, can't complain."

"Oh, that's great. I hate it when it gets too busy and then..." I flail my arms and babble words loudly... "You feel like this."

Alex rolls his eyes. "Right."

"I've had a lot of questions already—who do you usually run them by?"

Alex freezes in place.

I don't think I can get much out of him. Not because he's unfriendly, but because I have a feeling he knows nothing about who's really behind this. It's like a Ponzi scheme where no one knows who the mob boss is.

"Alex?"

"I need to be careful. I get in trouble if I talk too long." He whispers.

I fidget in my spot. "Oh, no. Sorry, I don't mean to get you into trouble."

Alex looks over his shoulder in the camera's direction, then looks back at me. His face is a shade paler, and his eyes wider. "Enjoy your lunch. I've gotta go now. I'll come get you soon, okay?"

Alex bolts for the door and disappears.

I'm still standing there, my heart sinking. Did I upset him? It just goes to show that he might have challenges of his own, yet he still does his job as best he can. The thought lingers longer than it should.

Are the people he works for evil? The question feels dramatic, even paranoid, but it won't leave my mind.

And then it hits me: I didn't even get the chance to ask about the books.

SEVENTEEN
RACHEL BROWNING

Alex is either too afraid or has something to hide—I can't quite decipher which.

Whatever it is, secrets seem to abound here. And now that I think about it more, Josh never seemed to reveal who the organizer of this whole thing is. Would he have said the person's name if I'd asked? The mastermind behind the prize —someone with too much money, someone who wouldn't even feel the loss of six million dollars.

Someone with an ulterior motive?

It's easier to accept what I was expecting. I thought this would be simple, manageable—but it's anything but. Everything I anticipated feels like a cruel joke.

Maybe I shouldn't care. Maybe my only concern should be living day by day and seeing this challenge through until the money hits my account. That's the whole deal, right?

The thought barely settles before Alex comes around shortly after lunch to let me out of my room.

He doesn't say anything; just stands by the door and watches me walk by.

We do the same as yesterday: I plod behind Alex through the hallway, in deep silence. We take the stairs again, which strikes me as highly odd, because there is an elevator on my floor. I don't ask; I keep following Alex.

He opens the door to the stairway, walking fast like he means business.

"Hey, Alex." I call out to him while I catch his stride.

He glances over his shoulder. "What?"

"I'll be honest," I'm looking at the dirty walls and stairs with cracks, and cobwebs hanging from the ceiling. "But this place doesn't feel like a luxury hotel."

Alex halts, turns around and shoots daggers from his eyes.

I stop, a short step behind Alex, fear coursing through me. Alex's eyes are something you'd see in a horror movie: like they belong to someone who's about to kill you.

"How dare you?" He says through his teeth.

"Oh, sorry, I didn't mean to..."

"You're here for the chance to win millions, and you're complaining? What the hell is wrong with you?"

I flinch. "Sorry, I didn't mean to..." my words trail off.

Alex resumes his walk, stomping like an angry kid. I follow a few steps behind him, my pulse still rattling in my ears. I replay the moment over and over, searching for the exact second I crossed some invisible line. It wasn't what I said—it was that I noticed. That I questioned the story I'd been handed. There's something dangerous about seeing the cracks, about naming them out loud. People like Alex don't want honesty; they want obedience, gratitude, silence. And frankly, it makes no sense since he's just the delivery boy.

I swallow the rest of my thoughts and keep moving, reminding myself that apologies are sometimes less about being wrong and more about surviving what comes next.

We arrive at the lobby.

It occurs to me for the first time the hotel looks small. All I've seen are the lobby, the pool, and the spa. The rest remains a mystery.

Alex leaves me standing behind; he doesn't bother so much as to tell me he is going to summon me in a couple of hours.

The Frankenstein man at the front desk is there, assisting someone with checking out. A sigh of relief washes over me. There are other people at the hotel.

I sit in a lobby chair, waiting for the person checking out to leave so I can have a word with him.

He looks so animated, happy—the type of person a luxury hotel would be happy to employ. He also looks a lot more rested: his eyes are not bloodshot, and he just looks lighter. Happier.

As soon as the person leaves, he spots me sitting in the chair, fear settling in his eyes immediately.

He turns and walks away from the front desk, disappearing from view.

What's he so bent out of shape about?

Seconds later, he's back, standing stiffly behind the desk. Something about him has shifted. The easy smile is gone, replaced by a tight, wary look—like I've flipped an invisible switch in his mind.

I stand up and approach the front desk. "Hey." I do my best to sound casual.

Frankly, ever since I realized I hadn't brought my anxiety meds, I've been feeling more self-conscious about my feelings and less like myself. It's like an out-of-body experience, observing myself surviving.

"Yes?" his voice is curt.

"I haven't caught your name..."

He cocks his head, squints his eyes. "I'm George."

"George!" I repeat. "Nice to meet you, George."

He says nothing in return.

I fidget in my spot, bouncing from foot to foot. It's awkward situations like this one that make my heart race.

"Listen, George. I went to the pool area yesterday, and... you know, it was strange that the spa rooms were locked and the pool empty. Is there an area in the hotel that has many people? You know, like a bar?"

George lifts his arm and points his index finger in the

corner's direction. I turn around and see the double door I hadn't seen before. It sits there obscurely, blending in with the rest of the wall, you can never tell the door is actually there.

I tap my palm against the desk. "Would you look at that! A door," I chuckle and look at George, who's staring at me with unblinking eyes. His lack of expression is unnerving.

I tap both of my palms against the desk this time. "I'll be on my way now. You have yourself a great day, George."

His face scrunches in repulsion.

I turn around and head for the door. What is it with Alex and George? They both move through the day like disgruntled employees, as if every day is a bad day. I wouldn't be surprised if both are jealous, knowing why I am here.

I swing the double doors open and find myself in a short hallway, leading to another double door. I open it, and behind the door, there is a large room adorned with multiple round tables. At each table, there are people eating their food, and not talking. Just staring at their plates. And what's more surprising is that every single person sitting at each table must be over eighty.

"What the fuck." I whisper.

Not one person notices my presence even though I am within earshot and eyesight of most of them.

In the far corner, there is an L-shaped bar. At least that. There's no one sitting at the bar. Completely empty.

On one wall, a large sign flashes DO NOT DISTURB.

It strikes me as strange. I can picture it hanging from a door-knob, but here—out in the open—it makes little sense, unless there's a good explanation.

The bartender sees me, smiles, and waves at me. Things around here are awfully strange and uncomfortable, but the sight of a friendly face puts me at ease.

I stride to the bar and sit in a chair at the very end.

The bartender places a napkin in front of me carefully, precisely, as if there's a correct way to do even that. He's middle-aged, maybe late forties, with neatly combed hair and a smile that looks practiced rather than natural.

"What can I get you?" he asks.

"Water," I blurt. Alcohol feels like a terrible idea right now, although I could use a drink just about now. But my nerves are already frayed enough.

He nods and turns away. I watch him fill the glass with steady hands, the way he doesn't glance toward the dining room even once. Behind me, the room remains eerily quiet—no clinking silverware, no murmured conversations. Just the faint scrape of forks against plates.

I slide off the barstool slightly and turn in my seat, taking another look at the diners.

They all sit too straight. Their faces are slack, vacant, like they've learned to eat without tasting. One woman lifts her fork in slow motion, bringing it to her mouth again and again, never once looking up. Is there even any food on that fork? She's too far for me to see. A man across from her chews endlessly, his jaw working as if he's forgotten why he started.

A chill crawls up my spine. This place resembles a retirement home more than a luxury hotel. Or it has to be just a strange coincidence for all this to be happening at once.

"Here you go," the bartender says, setting the glass in front of me.

"Thanks." My voice sounds small to my own ears. I take a sip, the water icy cold, grounding me just enough to keep my thoughts from spiraling completely out of control.

I lean in closer to the bar. "Busy place," I say lightly, gesturing behind me.

The bartender's smile falters just for a second. Barely noticeable. But I see it.

"They keep to themselves," he says.

"That seems obvious." I force a chuckle. "Is this, like, an assisted living outing or something?"

The bartender doesn't find my quip amusing at all—doesn't even crack a small smile.

He wipes an already spotless section of the counter. "Nah. They're visitors from a few towns over. Concord. They have an activity group and come here every month for lunch. They rent this dining area."

I study his face, waiting for more, but he doesn't elaborate.

"Oh, okay." Not sure if I've dug my own grave, but I keep conversing. "Can I ask you something?"

He pauses, then nods. "You just did." He smiles. "But go ahead. Ask another."

My fingers curl around the glass. The bartender seems like the most approachable person so far, friendly even with a hint of stiffness. Maybe he will give me the answers I want. I have so many, but I start with the basics.

"Why is there a DO NOT DISTURB sign on the wall?"

He gazes at the sign and shrugs. "Some people tend to disturb. We don't tolerate disturbance around here."

What kind of disturbance is he talking about to warrant the intrusive sign on the wall? I don't ask. Instead, since he's friendly enough, I finally voice the question that's been gnawing at me since day one. I lean forward and whisper, "Is there a reason we're not allowed to use the elevator going down?"

That does it.

He looks up sharply, eyes darting—not to me—but toward the double doors I came through.

"You shouldn't ask questions like that," he hisses.

My stomach drops. "Why?"

Just as he's about to answer, Alex appears out of thin air.

"Hey, your time is up. Let's go back to the room."

I look for a clock, but there isn't one in sight. "Really? I've been out for two hours already?" I feel panic coming over me.

When Alex takes me under my arm and pulls me up, I

glance at the bartender once again, and he's looking at me frozen in place, wide-eyed.

"Let's go." Alex repeats. Something sinister has settled in his eyes.

I get up from the chair, but I can barely move.

This could be my sign to throw in the towel and leave this place.

EIGHTEEN
RACHEL BROWNING

We take the elevator up. Just like yesterday. In dead silence.

Alex glances at me a few times, shaking his head slightly, as if I've already disappointed him—though I do not know how.

When the elevator dings and the doors slide open, Alex bolts down the hallway, moving fast, almost frantic, like he's being chased by something only he can see.

He unlocks my room and tells me he'll see me at six, when he drops off my dinner. No goodbye. No eye contact.

I step inside. The usual silence greets me, broken only by distant traffic humming far below. The door closes behind me. Locks.

Maybe I should make a plan. Some kind of strategy to survive my stay here. The suite is spacious, luxurious, but it feels like it's tightening at the edges as time goes by, shrinking around me.

I wander aimlessly until something white on the nightstand catches my eye.

A small rectangular piece of paper, folded neatly in half.

I don't remember putting it there. Then again, with everything happening, it's possible I don't remember a lot of things.

That thought unsettles me more than it should.

I step closer and pick it up. The paper is warm, as if it's been handled recently. I unfold it.

The handwriting is mine. There's no mistaking it. Teachers used to nag me about my letters—how my S's leaned the wrong way, how my T's wobbled like they couldn't stand on their own.

I read the note out loud.

STOP LEAVING THE ROOM.

"What?" I whisper.

My heart stutters. The words feel less like advice and more like a command. A warning. As if I wrote it knowing something I no longer do.

I turn toward the dresser, suddenly desperate to see the rules again—the piece of paper that was there yesterday, grounding me in some version of reality.

It's gone.

I freeze, staring at the empty surface.

No, that's not right.

I tear through the room, checking every flat surface first, then yanking open drawers, one after another. My movements grow frantic, sloppy. I check the dresser twice. Then, a third time.

Nothing.

A hollow sensation opens in my chest.

Was there ever a list of rules? Or did I invent that, too?

I look down at the note still clutched in my hand, my handwriting screaming at me from the page.

If I wrote this... If I warned myself... then maybe the real question isn't why the rules are gone.

It's what happened the last time I didn't listen.

I slowly fold the paper back up and set it on the night-stand, exactly where I found it.

Then I sit on the edge of the bed and wait—afraid to leave the room, and even more afraid of what staying might cost me.

By the time Alex shows up, I've racked my brain a million times about the note and the rules. Did someone come into my room and arrange things? Someone who knows me well. And my handwriting.

That's almost impossible.

I can't shake this feeling. My longing for the outside world—my shitty house and prospect-free life—intensifies with every passing minute. Sure, I'm not a quitter, but quitting becomes a real possibility when things start appearing out of thin air and nothing makes sense. Alex can't explain any of it. It's like he's part of a scheme someone else designed, plugged in only to execute it.

So, essentially, I ask myself: can I trust Alex? I probably can't. Not with the way he's acting.

ALEX COMES LATER that day to drop off the dinner tray. He's whistling a tune as if he has no care in the world.

"I'll see you tomorrow morning?" He's on his way out as soon as he drops off the tray.

I am still shaking from finding the obscure note in the room.

"No, wait." I say. "I have some questions for you."

He straightens up, seems suspicious. "Questions? What is it?"

"What happened to the piece of paper with the rules? It was sitting on the dresser, and now it's gone."

He scratches his head and gazes at the floor before his eyes meet mine. "The rules?"

"Yes. The rules. Did the room keeper take it?"

Alex gives me a half-smile. "There's no room keeper here, Rachel. I am the room keeper. You're looking at it."

"Oh. What did you do with the note?"

He takes a single step forward. "Nothing." We stare at each other for a while—it's eerie. "You don't need those rules anymore. And if I were you, I would really stop asking questions."

Alex leaves the room, slamming the door behind him.

His abrupt departure sends my anxiety through the roof. My heart is palpitating so fast, it feels like it's going to jump out of my chest.

"Oh, shit."

Is this the new normal—Alex ghosting me? Or is my memory tricking me, rewriting things so I can survive?

I lie in bed and stare at the ceiling, letting the darkness press in.

I weigh my options. Can I be the bigger person and ignore the strange circumstances I'm stuck in? Or should I cave and walk away from all of this? People aren't meant to be alone for this long.

When Mom was alive, she'd come to my room just for company, never giving herself a single hour of solitude. With her, it wasn't surprising. Dad, on the other hand, was always on the road, always busy. At night, he'd stop by his favorite bar and drink until he couldn't walk. How much he spent on taxis, God only knows.

I'm starting to think I am more like Mom.

I'm thinking: how long can a person survive without air? Not long. A few minutes, maybe less if panic takes over. The body knows before the mind does. It fights. It claws. It begs.

Without water? A couple of days. Three, if you're lucky. Your mouth dries first. Your thoughts follow. Everything becomes smaller, more unbearable .

Food is different. You can last a week. Longer, even. The body eats itself quietly, like it's trying not to make a fuss.

I catalog these facts the way some people count sheep.

And then there are other humans. How long can you survive without them?

Technically, a lifetime. People do it all the time. They lock themselves away, build routines that don't require conversation, convince themselves silence is peace. But surviving isn't the same as living. Not really.

Without people, there's no one to witness you. No one to tell you that you exist when you start to doubt it. No one to notice when something is wrong—when you stop eating, stop sleeping, stop breathing the way you should.

I think maybe we last the longest without humans. But we don't fare well.

Something essential thins out. And once it's gone, I'm not sure it ever comes back.

Roger looks concerned. He wants to talk about something. I can tell just from the look on his face it's a big problem whatever he wants to talk about.

Did he get the call that William had been discovered dead?

He twirls his fingers, staring at them as if one wrong move might give him away. He finally looks up.

"I just listened to the voicemail message," he says.

"Voicemail message?"

"Yes. A voicemail message." He repeats.

I'm prepping myself mentally. Bracing for the news.

Finally, he's about to tell me everything. Make a confession. Tell me he's ready to walk into the police station.

I believe there's a part of Roger that wants to live with a clean conscience. Because, he hasn't always been like this: on edge. My stomach flutters with nerves. I already know what he's done, but I'm primed for a reaction where he'd never suspect I already knew. There's something fucked up about people who know things and pretend not to, using it to their advantage. I don't want to be that person.

But I am when it comes to witnessing a murder.

Roger says something entirely unexpected.

"It was from your therapist."

I flinch. "My therapist? Why would my therapist call *you?*" Fear runs down my spine. My therapist, Stan Conley, is a middle-aged man, one I like, but I am not so sure anymore.

I trusted Stan. I really did. He was the kind who would listen intently, then offer advice with just enough empathy to make you feel safe.

What did he have to discuss with Roger?

"Why? Because I'm listed as your emergency contact. Doh."

Roger can't resist sarcasm. I roll my eyes. "I didn't mean that. What did he have to discuss?" I say through my clenched teeth.

It can't be any good if my therapist took the time to call Roger and share his concerns.

Roger looks around the room and leans forward. "He tells me you're acting out again. He says you could be a danger to yourself and others."

I don't understand what Roger means. For a moment, I don't believe him. Nothing out of the ordinary has happened. I've gone to my sessions. I've said what I'm supposed to say. But being accused of posing a danger to others crosses a line I didn't know existed, and one I won't accept.

"What the fuck, Roger," I say. "That's total bullshit, and you know it."

I don't think my therapist called at all. Roger is lying. He just killed William, so he's deflecting. He's trying to push me away. We've gone down this path again. He has done the deed; I just don't know why.

Now I wonder if he's filing for bankruptcy at all. It could just be an excuse to get rid of me. This is what I don't appreciate about Roger. He treats me as if I'm a complete fucking idiot. And now—I am the problem. Not him. Not after we tried to work out our issues for the millionth time.

I cock my head. "Roger, is there something you're not telling me?"

He straightens up in his seat and takes a sip of water. Slams it down against the table. "What do you mean?" he finally says.

I scoff. "Really? You don't really think I saw what you did at the office?"

"Felecia..." he whispers. "I don't know what you mean, but you really need to stop this. Okay?"

I laugh. "You killed William. Didn't you? You pushed him down the stairs.... the poor, helpless man in a wheelchair and now you pretend everything is fine?" Now I'm boiling with anger. My voice rises in a pitch. Roger is getting angrier. "What the fuck is wrong with you, Roger? Why do you think you're perfect?"

The waiter comes by and asks if we want anything. Roger shakes his head impatiently, and as soon as the waiter leaves the table, he turns to me. "You're losing your fucking mind." He says. "I love you, but you need to get a grip of yourself. You get it?"

I've seen Roger's anger many times, but he has never necessarily directed it at me with such intensity.

"Come on, just admit it." I whisper loudly through my clenched teeth.

Roger sets his eyes on me. "You are fucking insane."

TWENTY

RACHEL BROWNING

DAY 3

Something wakes me up in the middle of the night.

It could be early morning—I'm not sure. Whatever jolted me awake feels like it grabbed me by the throat and tried to choke the life out of me.

But, as always, it's just a nightmare. Still, it feels as though someone shook me with all their might to force me awake.

Ever since Roger and I split, my nightmares have returned. Those heavy, ugly dreams that haunt me like a fucking monster.

In my dream, I got a text message from my mother.

A message from her popped up on my phone saying, "Where are you?"

Her face is hollow. When I look at her, I'm staring straight into the bottom of a casket. Her mouth moves, but there's barely a mouth left—only maggots and dirt shifting where words should be.

Even in my dream, I wondered how my mom could text me from her grave. That's the part of the nightmare that your subconscious doesn't dig deep into.

When my mother died, cell phones were not up for general consumption. We had a single rotary phone at home and Mom's vocal cords to call me in when I was outside playing with the neighborhood kids. If I'm to venture a guess, the phone in my dream is the symbols for what I am missing now: connection with the outside world.

Besides, by now, Mom's body has turned into a skeleton. No flesh.

Dreaming about her isn't new. But she was never part of a nightmare—not until tonight. She always appeared in beautiful dreams, showing me nothing but brittle affection.

I am drenched in nightmare sweat. My breathing is shallow as I still shake off the dream.

I sit up and gaze through the window—the sky is bruised with stars, and the more I focus, the more stars materialize.

And then—something unexpected happens.

I hear voices.

They are not coming from the outside.

It's like there is someone on the other side of the door, whispering a story. Part of me feels excited I am not here alone—at least not in this space, this time—but fear runs through me when I wonder who it is out there and their intentions.

I muster strength and tiptoe to the door. I place my ear next to the door, and, to my surprise, the voice stops as soon as my ear touches the door.

It won't work, I know, but I pull the doorknob in case Alex left the door unlocked after he delivered dinner last night. The door is locked. I step away from the door when the voice returns—that steady whisper like it's coming from the bottom of a barrel, asking for help.

There's no way I can make out what it says, what it wants.

A hollow, guttural laugh comes from the other side. Not from the other side of the door. From elsewhere.

I walk along the walls, my ear pressed hard, as if to find the voice like it's a magnet. As I move forward, it gets quieter until the sounds come to a screeching halt.

That's it. No more voices. No laughter.

For a second, I wonder if I imagined it all, because, being alone on the floor, I don't see where the voices would come from, and especially at this time of night.

I look at the camera, the red-light flashing. But the frequency has changed. It's a rapid, jittery flicker now, not the slow, steady pulse that appeared every three seconds.

Not sure what that means, if anything. Perhaps these cameras act differently at night. Maybe there's an ultraviolet component getting activated... to see me at night.

Not sure. And I don't know how to feel about it. Afraid? Relieved? Determined to decide what's next?

I go back to the door and knock slightly. "Anybody out there?" my voice is uncertain, but the curiosity carries me on.

Nothing.

"Hello?"

Dead silence.

It's all pointless. I go back to bed, wondering if it's just a TV blasting from a building across. Unlikely, but all possibilities cross my mind.

I wish I could check the time, but now I've realized it's become a strange concept. A commodity. Silence permeates the room. And somehow, despite the spike of adrenaline making me extra alert, it finally puts me back to sleep.

WHEN I WAKE, the sun is already high. A tray of food sits on the table.

One corner hangs over the edge, as if it's trying to escape. Breakfast has been delivered, yet I never heard the door open or close. Did Alex come by on time?

The day is brutally bright with not a single cloud in the sky.

There is a prickling sensation of anxiety running through me, and for the first time since I arrived here, I don't feel like getting out of bed. The weather doesn't help. The sunshine beckons and reminds of things back home—hiking with my best friend, Julie, getting together with friends for lunch, soaking up the Nevada sun. It's like happiness equated with the sunshine—always plenty.

This was all before Roger and I started seeing financial hardships. My hangouts got reduced to hiking with Julie—a free activity—only to spend the entire time bitching about Roger losing it.

It would be nice to walk around Boston. When Roger came to visit, he'd always come home with a renewed sense of purpose. It was as if the city gave him the hope no other place could.

Julie. What's happening with Julie? I should check up on her.

I search for my phone aimlessly, tapping the covers and the bed beside me, looking over my shoulder to see if maybe I moved it to the nightstand, when it hits me: I don't have my phone.

"Ugh."

Frustration bubbles inside me.

Now I remember that I never told Julie I would come here and spend an entire month with no contact with the outside world. I can imagine her calling me persistently only to have her calls landing in my voicemail box.

There are only two phone numbers I've memorized: Julie's and Roger's.

Might as well forget Roger's, but Julie's? I've known her since I was sucking on a pacifier and learning how to walk.

She will be worried sick.

I swing my legs off the bed and pace back and forth around the room. My anxiety is through the roof, and I'm hating myself for forgetting my anxiety meds. I practically live off those.

I'm feeling so dizzy. I pray to God I don't pass out. I am only steps away from the camera, and I suppose I could stand still for ten seconds to signal the urgency, but instead, I turn around and dash to the bed and crash.

A raw feeling overwhelms me. Hot tears stream down my face, and my whole body convulses from the shaking. Now I wonder if this is a good idea at all. Maybe I should tell Alex I quit and leave the hotel, fly back home.

The pressure is unbearable—you never know how hard something is until you get into the situation. And this here, I don't know if I can take it any longer.

"Are you okay?"

I open my eyes and see Alex hovering above me. His pillbox hat sits crookedly on his head, and he looks like he hadn't slept all night.

I wipe my face with the back of my hand. "Yeah, yeah."

"You don't look okay." He says it as a matter of fact.

"Listen, Alex." I sit up straight while still gathering my wits. "I don't think this arrangement will work out. Can you please tell your boss... whoever it is, to let me go?"

Shock and fear cross his face. It's as if I told him I was going to jump out the window for fun. (Still can't figure out how to open it.)

"I... I wouldn't do it if I were you." He whispers.

"But I want to! I can't do it anymore!"

"Listen. I'm not supposed to tell you this...," he continues with a whisper... "but it really gets easier as time goes by. They don't want you walking out early. It messes with... whatever this is." His eyes dart to the camera in the corner, then back to me. "Just keep your head down, do what they say, and don't draw attention to yourself. It's safer that way."

His voice cracks on the last word, and for the first time since I met him, he looks genuinely afraid—not of me, but of whoever might be listening. He straightens suddenly, his expression snapping back into that cold, neutral mask.

"I'll bring your lunch at one," he announces louder, as if rehearsed, then turns on his heel.

"No, wait!" I plead. "I need your help. Please."

"What is it?"

"Can you please call my friend, Julie, and tell her where I am?"

Alex just stares at me. I'm about to pull on his coat, but he moves his arm out of my way.

"Please, Alex. I can give you her phone number. Just tell her briefly where I am and what I'm doing here. I know she's worried..."

Alex rolls his eyes. "Fine."

I give him her phone number, and he repeats it out loud several times so he can memorize it. I can only hope it will stay in his memory long enough until he's ready to pick up his phone and dial Julie.

After he rehearses long enough, he turns to leave again when I call after him. "No, wait?"

I swear I've never sounded so desperate in my life.

Before he turns around to face me, he passes a quick gaze toward the camera, then curtly says. "What?"

"I forgot to ask you yesterday about books. I'd love to have some books. Josh told me I could order anything I wanted. I'm assuming that includes books?" Alex cocks his head, listens intently. "Is that... is that right?"

"Yeah, I suppose I could do something about it."

"You could?" my voice quivers.

"What do you usually read?"

I feel my cheeks blush. "Oh, I'm not too picky, you know. Anything would do."

His demeanor changes, and his face brightens. He doesn't look like the same person at all. "Do you read indies?"

"In... indies? I don't know what that is."

My ignorance is astonishing, even to me.

"Indie authors? You know, the ones who publish their own books?"

"Oh... no, not really."

He shrugs. "There're so many good ones out there. To be

honest, I enjoy reading them a lot more than trad published ones."

I do not know what any of that means, but I nod in agreement. I don't want to make myself a bigger fool by saying something stupid than I already have.

"I'd highly suggest JD Setzer, John Randall, Jessica Sorensen." Alex speaks as if he's in a trance. "All great indie authors. Oh wait, and I just realized all of their first names begin with the letter J. It's just a coincidence, I guess." He chuckles, more to himself than with me.

"Okay, I'll read anything. Please, just bring me some books before I lose my mind."

Alex stares at me for too long before he finally says. "See you soon."

He strides through the room and bangs the door behind him.

He's about to call Julie and bring me books later.

For the first time since arriving, things seem to be shifting. I just don't know which direction.

Something is wrong.

Alex never comes to set me free for my walk.

I'm almost sure it's been longer than an hour since he stood there, in the middle of my room, telling me all about indie authors. Perhaps I'm not in the best position to measure the time without a clock, but I'm almost positive it's been long since he dropped off the food.

Did he have time to call Julie? Oh, gosh, what if they got into a long conversation and maybe she said more than she should have? Or maybe he quit because I pressured him too much to do things for me? Maybe he got caught? Maybe someone on the other side of the camera knows what I asked for?

If he had quit, it could have been all my fault.

I don't know if part of the rules is that no one can be contacted on my behalf while I'm here. But that would be such a silly rule, since I am still disconnected from the world.

Oh, gosh.

I pray he didn't quit. I pray I didn't get him into trouble.

And if he did quit, why didn't someone else come to get me?

I trot to the corner with the camera and stand there. My shoulders slump, and I feel I'm about to faint. Deep breath in. Deep breath out.

I raise my arm and wave. Once. Twice. Then suddenly, my arms flail violently as if I am having a seizure. A scream comes out of my mouth. I run away from the camera and grab the doorknob, but, of course, the door is locked.

I hate being here in this room with every ounce of my body.

I need to see someone now. I lie down in bed and curl myself into a ball, willing myself to calm down. Being without my anxiety meds is taking a real toll. My heartbeat thuds against the mattress, fast and loud, and every tiny sound in the room feels amplified—the hum of the vents, the soft rattle of pipes in the corner, even my breathing.

I squeeze my eyes shut, but it only makes the darkness tilt and sway. A tremor runs through me, and for a moment I'm terrified I'm going to pass out. I just need someone—anyone—to check on me. But no one comes. The silence presses in like a weight, and I can't tell anymore if it's the room or my mind closing in on itself.

I get off the bed, on my knees, and crawl to the mini fridge in the corner.

When I open the fridge door—sure enough—there is beer, vodka, wine... I never thought I would resort to this kind of behavior, but here I am.

I reach for the vodka bottle. Oh yes, the one Roger likes. Absolut. He seemed to think this particular brand didn't give him a huge headache the following day. I wouldn't know the difference.

The bottle's shut tight, so I gather all my strength to unscrew the cap. It's hard, and it tells me my muscles are already learning about how sedentary I've become, in only three short days.

Is it three?

Drinking alcohol isn't my thing, but today... today calls for it. Today is special. It feels like the last straw, and I need something to distract me, to help me lighten up my mind before I lose it completely.

After the fifth try, the cap finally loosens. I lift the bottle and take a big gulp, immediately feeling the warmth in my chest. The vodka rushes to my head, and I feel lightheaded. Light. Happy.

An involuntary laugh comes out of my mouth.

Wobbly, I get on my feet somehow, and they carry me through the room. I dance. And I sing *Unbreak My Heart* at the top of my lungs, spinning around. My happiness rises with every sip of vodka. For a second, I forget where I am. There's nothing but music blasting in my mind, out my mouth, and the rush of pure, stupid freedom flooding my veins. I twirl again, arms out, like the world finally cracked open just enough to let me breathe. The room tilts, the lights smear, and I don't even care. For one bright, ridiculous moment, I'm not trapped, not monitored, not falling apart. I'm just a woman drunk on cheap vodka and borrowed joy, belting out a song no one asked for.

The dizziness hits hard, slamming into me like a door I didn't see coming, and the fragile high splinters.

My stomach lurches. The room spins too fast now; the walls bend inward as if they're curious how far I'll fall. I reach for the dresser, miss it, and stumble backward, landing on the bed with a dull thud. The bottle slips from my hand and rolls onto the carpet, leaking a clear, sharp-smelling puddle.

I laugh again, but this time it sounds all wrong.

"Okay," I slur. "Okay."

My tongue feels thick. My thoughts blur together, sluggish and slippery. I try to sit up, but my head throbs like fucking hell, and nausea creeps up my throat. I swallow hard and press my palms into the mattress, grounding myself, waiting for the spinning to slow.

I close my eyes to curtail dizziness. It's not working.

Memories flash through my mind—dead bodies. Mutilated faces. My mother's smile. Roger's hand in mine. His smile soft at first. Then it twists into a grimace. His face warps: Medusa, a cyclops, Kraken. He squeezes my arm. Hard. Harder. Hardest.

I'm in profound pain. I scream at the top of my lungs.

Something inside me breaks.

"Why are you calling me fucking insane?" My hands are shaking.

Roger can be blunt, a jackass even, but he's never called me names like this. I've really triggered him this time.

He cocks his head, his bald forehead shining under the overhead lights.

"Why?" He shakes his head. "Your therapist told me you jumped on another patient yesterday."

I roll my eyes. It wasn't bad this time. She just fell to the floor and ended up with a bruise—nothing like she was in grave danger.

"Please," I say. "That bitch was being disrespectful again."

Her name is Roberta. She has this habit of preaching to the group, telling everyone how to fix their lives, when, in fact, she's the reason her husband is no longer alive. People like that don't get to lecture anyone.

Roger exhales through his nose and shakes his head again. "Listen to me. You need to control your impulses. It's enough you attacked me recently, but others? You can't let rage get to you like that. You'll get yourself into real trouble—and then what?"

I don't know.

I just don't want Roger to start counting everyone I've attacked so far. He has that habit, even though I've asked him more than once to stop reminding me.

I'm empty for words.

I'm already doing group therapy and individual therapy. One works better than the other, for obvious reasons. Group therapy is full of remorseful people who need help—like me. But when you put a bunch of us in one room and ask us to share, it's like sitting on a bomb, waiting for someone to strike the wrong match.

My therapist gave it a name. PTSD with dissociative or psychotic features. I wrote it down so I wouldn't forget, but I haven't. He said it's triggered by extreme stress. Isolation. Sleep deprivation. Sensory deprivation. None of it surprised me, considering what I had witnessed as a child.

Underlying cause: childhood trauma.

Medication can curb the symptoms, she says. But trauma doesn't disappear.

At some point, she told me I could no longer excuse my

behavior because of it. Trauma isn't a free pass. The vicious cycle—hurting others, then telling ourselves we had no choice—has to stop somewhere.

Roger knows all of this. I can tell he's losing his patience.

The call comes at a convenient time for him—when he hides something sinister.

There's a pause before he continues, quieter now. "I love you. But if you don't do something about this—if you don't get real help—we can't be together anymore. Do you understand me?"

My fingers are tangled in her hair. The familiar smell of the shampoo always grounds me and reminds me why I love Felecia. She feels familiar somehow, even though our personalities are complete opposites.

"I love your name. Felecia Mebane."

She chuckles.

She's having a good day today, even though the past few days were rough for her. This is why I decided to take her on a little trip, to get her mind off things. I won't lie, it can be tiring, but the benefit that comes with these last-minute trips is my own reprieve from reality.

I come closer to her and give her a smooch on her cheek.

She glances at me and smiles. "You just like the sex, admit it."

She puts her finger on my nose and pokes it playfully, like I'm just a little boy. I won't lie—sometimes, I do feel like a boy in her presence. Her seduction, her scent, her smile: everything about her drives me absolutely crazy.

We're lying on the couch in the living room, hot and sweaty. The place is open and spacious, not too bad for an Airbnb. Felecia wanted us to make a quick weekend trip, so I took her to Los Angeles. This time, we took the plane, because I didn't want Felecia to have a fit about how long it's going to take to get there.

And now we're here—always escaping from something.

The window is open, and the warm breeze reaches our naked bodies. It doesn't do much to ease the heat. But I feel good, despite the hot, sticky, persistent high temperatures permeating the air.

I take a puff of the blunt and hand it to her. "Don't tell me you don't enjoy it."

She takes it from my hand and laughs. "Well, I never said I didn't enjoy it, you goon."

Things are calm now between Felecia and me. Things are always better just after we've had sex and smoked a blunt.

"What do you think about going for a little ride?"

"A little ride?" she gives me the blunt back and stares at me. "Like, where?"

I prop my head on my elbow to face Felecia. "Well, you've been a good girl this year. I was going to take you for a little shopping. What do you say?"

Felecia gives me a small smile, then averts her gaze.

Something is swirling in her mind, I can just tell, but I don't expect her to tell me. She comes closer and gives me a kiss on the nose—of all places—and gets up from the couch.

"Where are you going?" I ask.

My eyes follow her around. Her delicate moves. Her hips swaying left and right. Her butt cheeks tight and so beautifully round. Her long hair cascading down her back like a waterfall. Gosh. She's a goddess. I am so lucky to have her in my life.

But I would feel luckier if Felecia could be less adamant about acting like a weirdo sometimes.

She doesn't say anything, even when I repeat the question. "Hey! Where are you going?"

She trots to the dresser, where her phone is charging, turns on the wireless speaker and takes her phone, looking down at it.

Soon enough, the music blasts through the speakers. *Dreams* by Fleetwood Mac.

Felecia puts her phone down next to the speaker and walks over to the vast and wide living room floor. She spreads her arms and closes her eyes and dances. First, she moves her arms above her head in waves, then places her hands on her waist and moves her hips around slowly.

Her hair flows naturally, following her body like a shadow. I sit up and lean against the couch cushions, watching Felecia unfold her beauty. She is completely unguarded, beautiful in a way that feels almost private.

I just want to grab her and bury my head in her bosom and stay there forever. But I watch her, mesmerized.

Let me be honest—this is a lot better than Felecia having an adult tantrum or calling me names. But goddamn it, I'm addicted to her, worse than being addicted to drugs.

Felecia sways in place, occasionally looks at me and smiles. She knows this is not her norm. She knows that smoking a blunt and having sex are two of the things that hinder the polluted mind. If she dances naked and acts like herself, the ugly memories will stay at bay.

The song skips. Next up: *Roxanne* by The Police.

I scoff at the sound of it. I hate this song.

Felecia looks at me and winks. She knows exactly what that song does to me. It's been stalking me longer than I care to admit.

No matter how many times I've told her I'm here for her, she never listens.

I plant my knuckles into the couch, ready to stand, ready to join her, when she throws her arm up, palm out.

"Don't."

She stops dancing mid-step, frozen, like something inside her just snapped.

"Felecia," I whisper.

The music keeps playing, and it shouldn't. It really shouldn't. My jaw tightens as the lyrics spill into the room.

"Don't you come near me!" she screams.

I raise my hands in mock surrender. "Okay. Okay. I won't."

She wraps her arms around herself and scans the room like she's looking for a way out.

I sit back on the couch and watch her dance. Her face glistens in the afternoon sun, and that's when I realize: Felecia is crying. But if I try to hug her, I know she won't let me.

She's crying, and instead of pulling her close, I feel the familiar tightening in my chest. Moments like this make me wonder how much longer I can keep cleaning up her moods.

The headache throbs with agonizing intensity.

That Absolut doesn't give you a headache is absolute bullshit. Maybe it wasn't an issue for Roger, but for me—I'm dying.

What's worse, I don't wake up in my soft bed. I lift my head just enough to check my surroundings. The toilet bowl sits beside my head; my feet are pressed against the bathtub.

Something wet coats the floor—something acrid. Repugnant. I sit up and realize my panties are soaked, the puddle beneath me unmistakable.

My urine.

"Oh, fuck!" I yelp.

I stand up and turn on the bathtub faucet, starting a bath. I should clean the floor, but I don't have the strength. My arms feel weak, as if I've been hauling bricks all night.

I strip and crawl into the tub. The warm water soothes

me, but the weakness is alarming. I can barely keep my head upright, so I rest it against the edge of the tub and close my eyes.

I don't remember how I got here. Or what I was doing last night. I vaguely recall opening the vodka bottle, feeling oddly pleased with myself. But ending up on the bathroom floor is a mystery. Was I crawling toward the toilet like a soldier on a battlefield? I probably needed to pee and fell asleep once I got here.

The bath revives me just enough to realize something obvious: drinking copious amounts of alcohol is irresponsible. It seemed like such a good idea last night. Always does when you think you need something strong to stimulate your emotions.

The water cools, snapping me back to the present. I drain the tub so I can get out more easily. My body trembles. I place one knee on the floor, lean across the tub's edge, and struggle to swing my other leg over.

Shit. I'm weaker than I thought.

That tracks.

I drank nothing but vodka last night, no food to balance it. My stomach growls in protest. I need to eat.

On my knees, I crawl back into the room on all fours. From this angle, the table is too high, so I pull myself up with both hands—and freeze.

There isn't just one food tray on the table.

There are two.

One holds last night's dinner—a stale-looking sandwich and a sad little salad. The other holds breakfast.

Have I really been out that long? Long enough to miss dinner and breakfast?

Was it Alex who delivered them? Why didn't he check on me when he found the room empty?

I throw on clothes, sit at the table, and devour the food. As I eat, the shaking in my arms begins to subside.

My head still feels heavy, but my thoughts are clear enough now. I'm done. Starting today, I want out. No amount of money is worth loneliness, anxiety, or the growing sense that this place is closing in on me like a fist. I need out. I need air. I need my life back—whatever fragments of it still exist beyond these walls.

I make noise on purpose—shift my feet, clear my throat—just to prove I'm still here. Nauseating. My high school teacher used to say humans are social creatures. I never truly understood that until now.

It hits me—I don't even know how many days it's been since I arrived. Five? Six? Maybe more. If I ask Alex, will he tell me? Or is that forbidden too, part of the no-clock rule?

I swear to God, they want me to break.

I rush to the window and twist the handle. Still locked.

"Argh!" I shout. "I just need some fresh air! For fuck's sake—give me some fresh air!"

Nothing happens. No response. No footsteps. No

rescue. The stupid camera does all the talking for the "higher-ups," whoever the hell they are.

I pace the room, but my movements are sluggish, as if I'm trudging through invisible syrup. My limbs feel detached, foreign—like someone else is pulling the strings, and their hands are tired.

The bed looks inviting. I collapse onto it and wait, hoping Alex might come by.

When I close my eyes, memories flood in. My old apartment. Sunlight filtering through thin curtains. A kettle whistling. Roger laughing in the kitchen while I burned toast for the hundredth time. For a moment, I can almost smell the coffee, feel the warmth on my skin, hear the clatter of our mismatched plates. It's so vivid my chest aches.

Then, I open my eyes.

The warmth evaporates, replaced by sterile light and a low mechanical hum. The memory feels borrowed—like it never truly belonged to me.

This isn't reacting anymore. It's taking over.

I'm not the same person without my meds. I can feel my mind slipping, spiraling into an endless loop with no exit, no clarity.

Strength comes in waves—not enough to feel normal, but enough to move. I get out of bed, stretch, and force myself through a simple routine. I walk the perimeter of the room again and again until something on the floor catches my eye.

A piece of paper lies near the dresser.

I bend down and pick it up. It's folded in half like the first note, but this one is crumpled, as if it's been handled too many times.

I open it.

The handwriting is mine. Of course, it is. And of course, I don't remember writing it—just like I don't remember the last one.

Maybe I wrote it drunk, but even that seems unlikely. I could barely lift my head last night.

As I read, my breath catches.

YOU SHOULDN'T TRUST HIM.

I gasp. What the hell does that mean? Who is he? And when did I write this?

I don't remember any of it.

The mystery terrifies me.

As I struggle to calm myself, a miracle happens. The door opens.

I sit up instantly as Alex rushes in, balancing a tray of food. His movements are frantic. His appearance—wrong. His shirt is untucked, his hat crooked, his eyes unfocused. He doesn't even blink.

He looks like someone fleeing something—and using my room as refuge.

"Alex!" My voice is sharp, too loud, like I'm trying to snap him out of his trance.

He freezes and stares at me, eyes wide with fear.

"What?" he whispers.

"I want out," I say quickly. "I'm done here. Please—tell whoever you need to tell. I can't take this pressure anymore. I need to go home. Be around people. Listen to music. Call my friends. Please. Just tell them."

He looks at me with pure contempt.

Then he turns and says, "Fuck you, lady."

"Wait... what?"

Before I can say anything else, he's gone. The door slams shut and locks from the outside.

It feels unreal. Like an alternate reality where I've been cast as the villain.

Will I ever wake up from this nightmare?

Not much time passes before Alex walks through the door again. I don't have a clock, but it feels like he was just here, leaving the food for me. This time, he's empty-handed, his face distraught.

He circles the room, stops at the dresser, runs a finger along its edge, and wipes away a thin layer of dust. He studies his finger, then wipes it on his pants.

He turns to me and smirks. "I hear you misbehaved yesterday."

I shake my head. "What? I don't know what you mean."

He takes a few steps toward me, then stops. "I just spoke with the bartender. He says you were disturbing his guests."

I scoff. "Excuse me?"

The bartender? The guy I pegged as the friendliest in this entire establishment? What a fucking asshole.

"That's right. He said you walked in there and caused a

serious disturbance. And what's worse, that group of folks is not coming back to the hotel. Ever."

I stare at Alex, his words echoing in my head.

I don't know what to say. I did walk in there, but I don't remember being loud or annoying.

"You know what that means, right?" His expression hardens. "I'll spell it out for you. The hotel will lose business and reputation. All because of you."

Shock courses through me. "Me?" I place a hand on my chest.

"Yes, you." He shoots daggers at me. "We can't allow that behavior here. Do you understand?"

"Look, I—"

He cuts me off. "We allowed you to leave your room, walk around, meet people, talk to them... but not this. This is absolutely unacceptable."

"But I—"

"I'm talking here," he snaps. "I'm sorry to say, but we need to change the rules a bit."

Fear rushes through me. This place has already taken a piece of my soul; I don't want—or expect—it to get worse.

"What are you going to do?" I whimper.

"Hm." He taps a finger against his lip, mocking. "Let me think. Oh, there's nothing to think about. You're no longer allowed to leave your room."

"What?" Fear shoots through me like a bullet train. "I'll be quiet. I promise. I won't say a word. But please... let me out. I can't be in this room all the time." I glance around and notice, for the first time, that my hands are shaking—but the room isn't moving. The panic is mine.

"Listen." His voice softens, like he's consoling me. "This isn't my decision. Remember—I'm just the messenger. You'll be fine." He smiles.

"No, I won't be fine!" I scream. "I want to leave the hotel. Now!"

Alex laughs. "I thought you said you weren't a quitter. Right? Why quit now when you're already several days in? Don't you know it gets easier as time goes by?"

He's messing with me. It can't get easier. Nothing ever does unless we flip our lives upside down and rip the fucking scum out by the roots.

"No!" I clench my fists near my face. "No!"

Alex steps closer and gently takes both my hands.

"Listen, dear. I want you to listen real good. Okay?"

I'm desperate. What choice do I have but to listen, even though I don't know if I can trust him—or this arrangement?

"Just tell me what you need—whatever you want—to make your stay more tolerable, and I'll get it for you. Okay?"

Hope flickers. "A clock?"

He scoffs. "Now be reasonable. That one's nonnegotiable."

Hope deflates.

Alex stares into my eyes like we're on a romantic date. I shake my head, tears blurring my vision. I wipe my nose with my hand, numb. This feels like something out of a horror movie.

Alex sits akimbo on the floor, elbows on his knees, head in his hands.

"Are you scared of death?" His voice turns ominous—its emotion hard to read.

"What?" I murmur.

"We all have to die. Have you accepted your demise, Rachel?" He tilts his head slightly, making him look even creepier.

I scoff. "I... I don't know."

Alex smiles and struggles to his feet. He slips his hands into his jacket pockets, the keys inside rattling. "You know, it's not that bad. Once you die, you won't even know it." His voice turns singsong. "But you do know the life you're living, so make it a good one." He smiles again. "Yes?"

I nod quickly, pushing hair out of my face. "Yes."

But deep down, I wonder if this is some kind of sign—one only Alex understands.

"Good," he says reassuringly. "Still anxious?"

I nod. "Yes. A lot." A whimper slips out.

"That's your biggest problem. If you want to live a good life, you have to let yourself feel completely. Stop blocking your emotions. When you do, anxiety creeps in. Anxiety is the catalyst of a miserable life. You know that, right?" He smirks.

Where does all this godly advice come from? I had no idea Alex carried this kind of wisdom.

He knows some things about me—but not even half of it.

He has no idea my mother was killed in front of me, that I've seen nothing but death since. Sure, anxiety can ruin your life—but life itself can turn it into hell. So who really wins?

"I guess." I don't argue.

"Now relax. Okay? Besides, you're not missing much on the other side," he chuckles.

Somehow, his unsolicited advice works. I thank him like he's a preacher and I'm nothing more than a pawn.

"Well, I'm on my way now. You rest up."

And just like that, he leaves.

My anxiety rushes back immediately.

When I open my eyes, darkness has already swallowed the city. How long I've been asleep, I can only guess.

Through the windowpane, I hear voices carrying from outside. It sounds like a fight—like someone is being attacked.

It feels like a bad dream, except my eyes are wide open. This isn't a mistake.

Curious, I stand and move closer to the window, scanning the desolate park below. The night is mostly clear, promising another sunny day tomorrow. Stars glitter in the distance, whispering their secrets.

Ha. Funny. When I was little, my mom used to hold me by the window while we searched for the moon. She'd ask, "Where do you think the moon is?" It was usually hiding behind a cloud, but my innocent mind had other ideas.

"It went to get me some candy."

Mom would chuckle.

Tonight, the moon is full and spectacular. From the twenty-first floor, I can only see so much below. The streetlights brighten the sidewalk and the curb. I focus on the pavement—and freeze.

What's unfolding before my eyes is unmistakable.

The sounds weren't a dream. This is real.

Two men stand on the curb. One is dragging the other, who struggles desperately to break free. He's trapped in his attacker's grip.

I strain my eyes, rubbing them, zooming in like a hawk. For a split second, I think I recognize the attacker.

He's wearing the same outfit—the pillbox hat, the hotel uniform. His slender frame is unmistakable.

Alex.

The man in his grasp is shouting, but no one comes to help. Alex always struck me as weak—malnourished, barely any muscle on his body. But now he's handling that man with terrifying ease.

Then I see it.

A knife in Alex's right hand.

He lifts his arm. It hovers for a moment before plunging toward the man's abdomen. Once. Twice. Thrice.

I gasp, my hands flying to my mouth. "Oh, my God."

My first instinct is to call 911—but I can't. I don't have a phone. No way to contact the outside world. Should I stand in front of the camera? Someone would come if I did... right?

Who would come?

It's always been Alex.

I don't move. I can't.

I'm glued to the window, unable to look away. My eyes refuse to leave the scene. I'm witnessing a young man's death from a safe distance, and guilt coils in my stomach.

The man collapses like a leaf falling from a tree.

Alex straightens, victorious, watching the body from above. He doesn't rush. He doesn't flinch. Like none of it is a big deal.

What a monster.

I never imagined Alex capable of something this horrific. When I first met him, he seemed good-natured—humble, even. But it's always the quiet ones you should watch. I should've known when he walked me to the lobby the other day—his darkness was closer than I realized.

God knows what he's brewing in that twisted mind of his while the world keeps moving on.

And then—

Every drop of blood in my veins freezes.

Alex turns toward the hotel. Stands up straight like a statue. Slowly lifts his head. His eyes find my window.

They lock onto mine.

He smiles.

Then he waves.

At me.

I duck instantly, squatting against the wall, gasping for air. Oh my God. Alex saw me. That monster saw me.

He looked straight at me.

My chest heaves as sweat slicks my palms.

How did he know I was there?

I try to steady myself. Breathe in. Breathe out.

Maybe I should stand in front of the camera—signal an emergency—but my body is glued to the floor. I can barely move.

What the hell is happening?

For a split second, I imagine Alex bursting through the door, that same smile stretched across his face, warning me to keep quiet. To tell no one. Where is he now? What did he do with the body?

On my knees, I inch back toward the window, slow and stiff, like a sloth. I peek out from behind the curtain, dread pounding through me.

The curb is empty.

No body. No blood.

Not a single trace of murder.

Something twists violently in my stomach. I force myself upright and bolt for the bathroom.

I try to sit up. The room tilts. I stay where I am.

Think, Rachel. Think, for fuck's sake.

Alex will be storming into my room any second—either threatening me to keep my mouth shut, or I'll end up with the same destiny as the man he just killed.

He's a smooth operator, this Alex guy.

One minute he's preaching to me about death and dying; the next he's sending someone to their own demise.

And the speed at which it all happened is unnerving.

Where's the body? What did he do with it?

It only signals that this isn't his first rodeo. For all I know, Alex could be a serial killer in disguise.

Does the hotel know?

I want to think, come up with a plan to face Alex, maybe even escape...

There's a sound in my ears—blood rushing, or maybe the echo of something louder. A shout. A thud. The sound of breath leaving a body too fast. I close my eyes again, and the Boston Common blooms behind my lids. Grass flattened by footsteps. Bare branches clawing at the sky. Alex's back, rigid. Someone else's shape folding in on itself.

I swallow hard.

I tell myself to think practically. That's what Alex says.

Let yourself feel.

Facts first. Panic later. I inventory my body. Arms sore. Legs shaky. Mouth: copper. My lower lip is split. I taste it again, just to be sure, just to be sure I'm alive.

I go to the bathroom to wash my face with cold water; that usually does the trick. Timid, I trot over to the bathroom, expecting Alex to come in with that creepy smile that disarms. Alex could be busy transporting the dead body to a different place right about now. Maybe he's looking for a dumpster hidden in plain sight. Or maybe he's going to toss it into the Atlantic Ocean for sharks to consume. If he is, and I hope that's what's happening, that will buy me some time.

I lean over the sink and look at my hands. They're clean. Why did I think they were covered in blood?

The memory won't settle. It won't do what memories are supposed to do—arrange themselves into before and after. There's only the middle. Alex lunging forward. A body hitting the ground. A sound like a dropped bag of groceries.

I didn't scream. I know that much. I remember thinking I should scream, and then not doing it.

I press my fingers into my temples. The pain spikes, sharp and immediate, and with it comes something else. Not the murder on the Boston Common. Something older.

The first time it happened, I was seven.

That evening, Dad came home late, and he got into a fight with Mom as soon as he crossed the threshold. I was in my room, my ear pressed to the door, listening. I couldn't tell what they were fighting about. I hoped it wasn't because I'd told Mom I wanted a cabbage patch kids doll and Dad didn't want her to buy it.

Ten minutes later, the cops showed up. Apparently, Mom had called them because Dad wouldn't stop shouting. I overheard unfamiliar voices—I assumed they were the police —then, at some point, a door slammed and the cops left.

Nothing happened.

Mom just got into more trouble.

"Why did you call the cops, you bitch?"

I could hear Dad screaming clearly now. His words echoed throughout the house, impossible to avoid even if I tried.

I shivered at his rage. Mom was probably scared to death, and even the cops couldn't help her. Dad's constant yelling must have worn her down—her self-esteem and confidence eroding slowly. Happiness gone. Why did he have to be like this?

In the back of my mind, I wondered if I could stop all the madness. Poor Mom didn't even yell back; she was like a sponge, absorbing Dad's insults.

I slowly opened the door and slipped out of the room.

I walked toward the kitchen, and that's when I saw it. This was why Mom didn't talk.

She was lying on the floor, helpless, while Dad was on top of her. Mom tried to escape his grip, but there was no chance of that. I stood frozen in the doorway, my eyes bulging at what I couldn't believe I was seeing.

Dad held a meat mallet in his hand and struck Mom's face again and again. Bones cracked. Blood splattered like a fountain. Dad grunted as he beat her to a pulp, like a lumberjack chopping wood for a fireplace.

He wasn't a lumberjack.

He was a murderer.

He had just killed my mom.

A whimper escaped my mouth.

Dad heard me and lifted his head, surprised to see me standing there.

"Go to your room," he said at first, calm.

I looked at Mom's dead body—her face unrecognizable, only her blonde hair still intact—and I couldn't move. It was too late to help her. It was all my fault.

Dad's face twisted with rage. "Go to your room! Now!"

I ran, but a deep sadness settled in my chest immediately. My mom was gone, and I already missed her.

Tears roll down my face. I sob. My body hyperventilates.

In between the sobs, my dad's voice comes into focus. He's on the phone.

"Yeah.... Hi... I've just killed my wife... Come get me."

I scream at the top of my lungs, "Fuck you! Fuck you, you motherfucking scum!"

Thank goodness he turned himself in after. The cops came to summon him. Even my father knew he'd get a life sentence, with no chance of parole. That's what happens when you let impulses lead your life. You can flip it inside out, upside down in a matter of minutes.

I've never felt sorry for my father, but I know he regretted what he did. One day, a letter arrived from his jail cell—a long-winded confession.

For all I know, he can burn in hell just like his letter burned in my fireplace.

I slide my legs out in front of me and try to keep straight. I make it. The mirror over the sink catches my reflection, and I flinch. There's a bruise blooming along my jawline, already darkening. I don't even know what caused it, but it's vicious enough that I can't ignore it. My eyes look wrong. Too bright, like water stuck behind a dam.

"Get it together," I say aloud. My voice cracks on the last word.

Alex. I need to think about Alex.

Why did he kill that man?

I grip the edge of the sink now, grounding myself. The tile is solid. The mirror doesn't change when I look away and back again. This is real. I am here. I pinch myself to make sure.

I think about the Common again. The way the shadows stretched across the path. The way Alex turned toward me. Did he say something?

My chest tightens. I can't breathe for a second, then another. I force air in through my nose, out through my mouth, counting the way I was taught.

There's a particular calm that comes right before. A narrowing. The world simplifies. Right and wrong become irrelevant. There is only movement and release.

I lower myself onto the edge of the tub. My legs tremble. I press my palms flat against my thighs as if I can pin myself in place.

I look down again at my hands. There's a faint ache in my knuckles now that I pay attention to it. It could be from the fall. It could be from anything. I curl my fingers into fists and then force them open.

The bathroom feels smaller. The walls inch closer. I open the door, needing space, light, something to anchor me to the present.

As I step into the room, a final thought slips in, quiet and insistent.

I have always been good at forgetting the moments right

after. The second where everything is still possible. The moment when it could have gone either way.

I am waiting for Alex to come into my room any second now.

But he never does.

Felecia stops dancing and bolts to the bedroom. Slams the door hard.

I would run after Felecia if I didn't know she wanted that.

But I know damn well she doesn't. She wouldn't want me near her right now.

I stroll to the kitchen and open the fridge, fetching a beer out of the middle drawer. The cap snaps open at my fingertips, and I take a big swig. There's nothing like a cold beer on a hot day and an extra sedative to relax my muscles.

Felecia is probably in the bedroom, curled up in the bed, crying, meditating... God knows.

I go back to the couch and sit down. Another sip. I'm tempted to turn the TV on, but it's Sunday and I'm not a huge fan of football. I know—my high school classmates always made fun of me when I told them I wasn't into it.

Interior design? It was for damn pussies and not manly men, and certainly, they always thought I was never a manly man.

Fuck them all.

Even at that age, I cared less about building an image and gaining muscle than about being a decent human being. Girls loved me for it. All I wanted was to protect them somehow, in my own way.

I sag further into the couch and take another swig of my beer. Felecia is still in the bedroom, and I don't dare bother her right now. Not like I haven't tried before. I've done it. It didn't end well.

The music keeps playing, but I'm too lazy to get up and shut it off. *Roxanne* is finally over, and the happier tune is on now.

Sweet Dreams by Beyoncé.

This one will pass muster with Felecia. She'd dance to it so many times, getting into a trance, forgetting the world as it passes by.

Every time she smokes weed, something dark triggers within her.

Actually, it's more like hot iron getting tossed into ice: her moods switch instantly, like a sweet dream or a beautiful nightmare.

It's more like a nightmare.

Like the time she woke up in hot sweats, gasping for air, shaking off her nightmare, clinging to me like a child?

That particular conversation...

My phone chimes. It doesn't chime much on Sundays. I usually turn it on vibrate, so I can get some peace and relax. But, right now, I don't mind. I could use some distraction.

I sit up straight, take another sip of my beer, and open my phone.

It's an email from William. My partner in crime.

I don't know what I'd do without him. I've known him for over a decade now. He's the reason our business has been flourishing. He's the reason I don't need to worry about my spending habits, about buying whatever Felecia desires under the sun, about making her happy, like it's the way to cure all her childhood trauma. I don't ask, I just do.

I just scored another big client.

Call me so we can discuss.

No, not now. Not on a Sunday. That's the line I won't be crossing.

Not when Felecia hides in the room and acts like it's the end of the world. Not when I'm high as a kite. Not that he would mind, but there's something to be said about being professional at all times, even on a Sunday, even with the partner you view as a father.

Felecia may storm in any second, so I want to be available to her.

I completely understand where she's coming from.

Trauma is not something you can shake off and tell it to fuck off. It seeps into your subconscious, crawls under your skin, tucks deep into your bones, parks in your central nervous system, and you learn to cope with it. Live a life as if it's not part of it.

It was like a typhoon took over their place, destroying everything in its path.

The stories Felecia told me.

What the fuck.

Felecia has these strange memory flashes—trauma doing its work.

And I can't help her. I really try.

She's standing by the door, all dressed up. A short black dress with matching stilettos and delicately applied makeup. She looks like she's ready to go somewhere.

She walks by the phone charger, grabs her phone and turns the music off.

"Go get ready. Take me out."

I will myself to walk to the bed.

But I change my mind.

Maybe I should stand in front of the camera for ten seconds. Ask for help. Emergency. It is an emergency, after all. I just witnessed Alex killing someone.

If I can only get there.

I muster all my energy and stand in front of the camera.

One.

Two.

Three.

Four.

Five.

Six.

Seven.

Eight.

Nine.

Ten.

I walk away. Did I do this right?

I wait.

Shortly after, the door opens. It's Alex. Cold spreads through my limbs, my pulse pounding so loudly I'm sure he can hear it. But I've braced myself for whatever comes next. I'll let Alex have it. I'm nothing special, really. Perfect prey— someone who wanted to get rich quickly, reckless enough to step into the wrong game.

I can't see him well—just the contours of his slim, tall body. The room is awfully dark, his shadow stretching across the wall.

A long, dark silhouette takes slow steps toward me.

"Can you turn on the lights, please?" I say.

He does.

He's standing by the door, looking disheveled. His hair is plastered to his forehead, like a badly fitted wig. His face is laced with concern.

"You need something urgently?" he asks.

"I just saw you." I'm risking my life by admitting this, but here's the raw truth: he saw me, too.

He cocks his head. "I don't know what you're talking about." His voice is harsh. "Is there something you need or not?"

"I saw you!" I scream. "I saw you!"

Alex shifts and takes another step closer.

"Don't do this, Rachel," he says. "Or the rules will tighten even more."

I SIT UP IN BED, disoriented, as if I just woke up from a bad dream. Outside the window, the stars are sparkling, and the silence seems permanent.

A funky smell jolts me awake; the smell that makes you run for your life and retch until there's nothing left inside. I curl up my nose, as if to dismiss the odor, but I can't help it. It's strong. Putrid. I get out of bed and block my nose, looking for the source. My feet first take me to the bathroom, but the bathroom is unusually clean, and there's nothing out of the ordinary.

I run back to the room and touch the walls like they have secrets to share. Maybe a dead animal is hiding in the wall, and its putrid odor has penetrated. The odor is becoming unbearable.

Tears roll down my face out of frustration. Fear.

"What the fuck is going on?"

It occurs to me maybe it was a piece of food leftover from my meals left to rot, but I see nothing in my vicinity. And what's more, there's no dinner tray sitting on the floor or on the table. Did Alex forget to deliver it earlier?

The urge to open the window and scream is bubbling. I run to it and try to open it—nothing again. I ball my hand into a fist and slam on the windowpane. A heavy growl escapes my mouth.

I pace around the room, half-wanting to smash the camera with its red light flashing at me like a million fucking snipers pointing at me. I raise my hand and flip the bird. "Whoever the hell is watching me right now, fuck you! Fuck you!"

Let them see my rage. I don't care anymore.

I didn't sign up for this. A place with no time and horrid conditions.

Something pulls me toward the door. I bang on it like my life depends on it—and it probably does. This place has become a trap, not what I envisioned when I agreed to this. I need to find out who's behind it all. And why.

"Can you hear me?" my voice cracks. "Open the door! Open the fucking door!"

I know it won't reach anyone. I am all alone on the floor.

The banging continues, balancing the dead silence in the room and on the other side of the door.

I place my hand on the knob and pull it when, to my surprise, the door opens.

I scoff. "What? The room has been unlocked the whole night?"

This discovery should make me happy, but it's unnerving. The door is wide open. Just another oddity that doesn't add up with anything. Did Alex forget to lock it up? Perhaps the rules have changed, but he hasn't bothered to tell me.

I slowly crack the door open, just enough to see the wall across the hallway. My senses heighten as I listen to sounds. Nothing.

The odor intensifies.

I curl up my nose, but the adrenaline is stronger than the odor. The curiosity pulls me outside; I weasel out of the room and step into the hallway, feeling a sense of freedom and dread at the same time.

Maybe I shouldn't be here, outside my room. Maybe this is a test to disqualify me and send me home.

The hallway—it doesn't look the same as the first time I stepped foot on it.

As I remember, the carpet was blue, and the walls were covered in wallpaper. But now, it looks like the carpet is more brownish, and the walls—I don't see any wallpaper. Maybe the light is just too dim—a single fluorescent bulb hanging from the ceiling, flickering in the middle of the hall-way. It's entirely possible it's distorting the view, warping the colors. Or maybe it's my memory that's slipping.

The hallway is longer than I remembered it. It's shaped like a semicircle, leading to two ends with exit doors on each side. Like in my nightmares. I look to my right, then to my left before I decide which direction to take. I glance back at my room once more—the room feels cold and empty from this angle. Hard to believe this is the place where I've spent the last few days pretending everything was fine, convincing myself the unease simmering beneath my skin was nothing more than exhaustion. Now, standing outside it, the truth presses harder: something is wrong, and it's getting harder to ignore.

Something urges me to turn right, my heartbeat thudding in my ears. I move quickly but quietly, fingertips gliding along the wall as if staying connected to it might keep me safe—might help me slip away unnoticed.

But that's wishful thinking.

Because just a few steps later, I freeze.

There's a surprise waiting for me.

A big one.

I scream.

There's something lying on the floor.

Looks heavy... long. A person. Most likely.

Fear runs through me. I hesitate to step forward, but maybe it's someone who passed out and needs help.

I stumble forward, slam my hand against the wall, and hiss out a breath. "Dammit—what—"

Everything inside me freezes.

I'm confident it's a body lying on the floor. Unmoving.

I kneel to get a better look, and I gasp when I see the familiar face.

Alex.

He is lying on his back. His eyes are wide open, staring at the ceiling with a blankness that doesn't belong to the living.

"Oh, my God," I whimper. "What the fuck."

For half a second, my mind refuses to process what I'm seeing. The pillbox hat is sitting next to his head. His pale blue uniform is rumpled; one sleeve is torn. His skin—God, his skin—is grayish, waxy, like someone drained the color from him.

"Alex?" The word comes out strangled.

He doesn't blink. Or breathe. He definitely doesn't move.

I nudge him, feeling like an idiot. Still doesn't move.

The putrid odor has to be coming from him. How long has he been lying here dead? Why didn't anybody notice? The front desk guy? Frankenstein. Where is he?

A cold rush sweeps through me, shaking my bones.

Panic strikes me like a heavy sledgehammer over my head. I stand up and run for the exit on my right. The flickering light seems like it's trying to give up and goes in and out, blurring my path.

I come to the end of the hallway. The exit door... it's right there. Heavy. Metal. The EXIT sign is red and lit, staring down at me. I try to push the door open, but it's locked. I bang hard against it—how long; I don't even know—but no one comes from the other side.

"Fuck!" I scream through a roar of tears.

I don't linger. I move on.

I try the elevator. The damn thing doesn't go down, only up from this floor, and I still don't know why. I slam on the

DOWN button, pushing it several times, but nothing happens. Not a single thing.

"Damn it!" I scream.

My feet take me to the other side of the hallway. I seem to think that it's the hallway with two exits, but when I get to the other side, there's nothing. I swear there were two exits before. Only an ice machine sitting lonely in the corner.

I whimper.

I can't stand the pressure of seeking a way out—it's turning into a nightmare.

With no luck, I storm into my room, leaving the body lying on the hallway floor, and stand in front of the camera. The lights are flashing, flashing, flashing...

I squint and clench my fists as I stand in front of it and count to ten. One, two, three... it's to ten I need to count to signal the urgency.

The count is up.

I move away from the camera and pace around the room. A scream comes out of my mouth. The only time I felt panic this intense was when I saw Roger that day, marked by blood and death.

If only I had my meds to keep cool-headed.

Oh, God. I keep thinking about Alex. How did he die? Then the worst thing crosses my mind, something a human should never consider: what if he didn't die of natural death? What if someone murdered him?

And whoever did... am I next? Or worse: was it me who

did it? Some kind of self-defense while in a blackout. I wouldn't be surprised. People have done it and then claim not to remember a single thing.

"Fuck this shit." Tears are relentless.

I pace around the room, glancing at the door, expecting someone to storm in and offer help. Enough time has passed for me to realize no one is coming. No helping hand.

Because that person is usually Alex. And now he's dead.

"Oh, my God!" I scream at the top of my lungs, feeling like I'm about to lose my consciousness.

I run for the door, but to my surprise, it's locked. I rattle the knob with madness and urgency, but the door stays locked.

How is it locked now? It was unlocked just minutes ago.

Nothing makes sense anymore.

I turn around and lean my back against the door, sliding down to the floor. Hyperventilating, my breath comes in ragged waves.

My eyes grow heavy. A black screen drifts over them.

I fight with everything I have to stay conscious, but the darkness is closing in fast. Before I can latch onto anything—anything at all—I slip under, and the world goes pitch dark.

Two rules for a happy life.

One: use things, not people. And two: love people, not things.

I can't say this is the case with me and Felecia.

I am almost fully convinced she's just using me for my money. God bless her soul.

By now, she's used to the special treatment, which I've availed it to her based on my goodwill. Felecia gets whatever her heart desires. When you're so broken, I guess you look to repair the patches of yourself in the most unexpected places: expensive jewelry, designer clothes, multiple pairs of Jimmy Choo shoes, trips to different parts of the planet at a whim.

Our interest is mutual. I can't fully blame her, because I've enabled her to ask for whatever she wants. She's addicted to things—that's what makes her happy—and I'm addicted to her. It's a match made in heaven.

I tell her I need to take a shower while she waits for me in the living room. She sits down in the recliner across the couch and purses her lips and studies her fingernails, playing with them, raising her eyes occasionally and glancing at me.

I'm finishing my beer, last drops, when Felecia suddenly puts her arms down and clenches for the armrest with tension in her shoulders. "I can't live like this anymore."

Her voice quivers; she looks like she's about to cry.

I cock my head. One thing about Felecia is that she's easy on the eyes but really fucking hard on the mind. There's always something.

"What is it, babe?" I say.

She shakes her head quickly. "I just... can't."

I watch her closely, the way her fingers curl into the leather armrest, the way her knee bounces like it's trying to escape the rest of her body. This isn't one of her moods—the dramatic kind that passes after a shopping trip or a glass of wine. This feels different. Heavier.

"Can't what?" I ask, keeping my voice calm. Gentle. The way she likes it when she's fragile.

"This," she says, gesturing vaguely between us. "The lies. I feel like I'm suffocating."

That word hits me wrong. Suffocating. As if I'm the one choking her, when I've done nothing but make her life easier. Better.

I stand and set the empty bottle on the counter a little

harder than necessary. "You're not suffocating," I say. "You're overwhelmed. Big difference."

She looks up at me then, eyes glossy. "You don't get it."

I smile, slow and patient. "I get everything."

Her default is always "suffocating." I swear, sometimes I want to shake the shit out of her and tell her to get it together.

She laughs weakly, a broken sound. "You always say that."

Because it's true. Because I see things she doesn't even realize she's showing me. The cracks. The need. The fear of being alone. She says she wants out, but I know her better than she knows herself.

"You don't have to live like anything," I say, stepping closer. "You live like this because you choose to."

Her lips part, like she wants to argue, but no words come out. Instead, she looks away. That's her tell. When she looks away, she's already lost.

I reach out and brush my thumb along her jaw, light enough to be comforting, firm enough to remind her I'm there. "You're safe," I tell her. "You're taken care of. That's more than most people get."

Her breath hitches.

She doesn't pull away.

"Look, let me get ready and take you someplace nice, okay?"

Felecia stares at me, but she doesn't confirm. By now, it's an expectation that I do something to make her feel better.

I stand up and give her a quick kiss on the top of her head. Her perfume lingers, and I inhale the sweet scent, feeling something shift inside me. She's so good at making me feel—and not all the feelings are good.

As I stand in front of the bathroom mirror, I am checking myself out. I'm thirty-eight years old. Still in decent shape. The six-pack is still there. The biceps are nothing to sneeze at. I like my fancy suits and shoes that turn heads around.

There's something that lingers in my mind nonstop: I want children. I'm still young enough to reproduce and to be a father. I'd love to have two, maybe even three, and pass on my business to my heir.

My balding head concerns me: my hair started falling off a few years ago, but that process sped up the last couple of years, like a middle-age man suddenly ending up in a hospice for the last straw of life.

I'm just hoping women out there like balding men. Women who aren't superficial and still want children.

But let's face it, Felecia is not it.

I can't have children with the person who can't get a grip on her emotions even in the simplest situations. She's a danger to herself and others. I need a woman I can trust. A woman who is sane enough to know that, once you have children, they become your whole world. You feed them. You raise them. You make sure they live and continue to live.

But that's just the beginning until they become aware of their existence and learn to love themselves.

Will Felecia be the kind of mother who will help them in that department?

You know what they say about trauma? Not only does it follow you for the rest of your life, but it can also sneak into the next generations. You can't really fool a child.

Unless someone puts a stop to it, untangles the chains, cuts them off. And that better be me.

People like Felecia don't walk away from comfort. They cling to it. And that can't sustain a relationship, even ones that thrived in the past.

I love this woman, but she might be right. I don't know how much longer I can take this.

There's a whisper calling me from under the bed. "Rachel. Rachel, get up."

I open my eyes, the sudden burst of sun offending them.

"Rachel, Rachel... wake up," the voice continues.

I turn onto my side and slowly slide across the bed to inspect beneath it, to see who's calling my name. Hanging off the edge of the mattress, I listen as the voice gets closer, still whispering. There's no one under the bed. Nothing.

The voices must be figments of my imagination.

I roll onto my back and reach for my head. The migraine. My skull throbs as if a band of drummers is marching through my brain.

"Ugh," I whisper.

Memories from last night surface. That I left the room briefly and wandered the hallway. One exit with a locked door. Through the fog, I reason that I'm trapped, with no way out, and I need to leave this place.

If I can.

A sudden flash jolts me more awake.

Alex.

That thought sends shivers down my spine. Dead Alex. His helpless body lying on the floor, his hollow, unmoving eyes staring at the ceiling. What happened to him? How did he die?

I find the strength to stand and walk to the door. Maybe Alex is still where I last saw him. I crawl the final steps and lean against the door, exhausted. There's no breakfast tray on the table. Will someone else deliver it?

I reach for the knob and turn it. It won't budge. Locked.

I twist it harder, left and right, but the door doesn't move.

How did I get out last night? Was it all a dream?

Drained, I force myself back to the bed and collapse.

"Rachel. Rachel..." the whispers continue.

"Who is it?" I raise my voice. "Who the hell is calling my name?"

A chuckle. An evil chuckle.

"What the hell is happening?" I clamp my hands over my ears and squeeze my eyes shut.

An image flashes through my mind—me falling off a cliff. A long, endless drop, my body cracking like an egg at the bottom of an abyss.

I'm losing it.

I've had visions before, but never like this. The voices. The vile images. I need them out of my head.

Get the fuck out of here.

But how?

The door opening makes my eyes fly open. The light is blinding.

"Ugh."

A man walks in. I see him only in my periphery; I don't look straight at him. Fear prickles down my spine. My chest feels heavy, my head on the verge of exploding.

"Are you okay?" the man asks.

The voice is familiar. The same voice I've heard since I arrived—the only one that's spoken to me here.

I look up.

A scream rips from my throat.

"Alex!"

He stands by the door, whole and solid, concern etched on his face. Same pale skin. Same eyes boring into me, as if he knows things he'll never say.

"Alex," I whisper. "Is that really you?"

My hands shake uncontrollably. He's here, in flesh and blood. But he should be dead. I saw him on the floor, eyes fixed on the ceiling, his skin turning paler by the second.

Alex flinches. "What do you mean?"

"I... I thought—"

"Here's your food," he interrupts. "It's lunchtime."

He's already set the tray on the table.

"Lunchtime?" My voice trembles. "It's not breakfast?"

"No, lunch," he repeats, shutting it down.

Have I slept that long? Through the entire morning?

I slide off the bed and crawl toward him. Walking feels impossible. I stop at his feet and look up. His slim body is rigid, unmoving, his gaze fixed on mine.

"What... what is this place?" I plead. "Please tell me."

He squints, irritated—or disturbed.

Alex says nothing.

"Please," I scream. "You need to get me out of here!"

"I brought you books," he says calmly, as if I'm not unraveling. He leaves and returns with a small stack. "Harsh Winters by John Randall. Keeping You Close by Jessica Sorensen. The Web She Wove by JD Setzer. That should keep you busy."

I barely glance at them. "I need to leave. Today."

Alex straightens, looming. "You're not going anywhere. The rules have changed."

I whimper. "The rules? What rules?"

"Why don't you stand up, Rachel?" He cocks his head. "Let's talk."

The words make my stomach drop.

I force myself upright, my body trembling. We stand face to face. His expression doesn't change.

He shakes his head slowly, like I'm a disappointment. And maybe I am.

"What is it?" I whisper.

For the first time, his eyes harden.

"You broke a rule."

My breath catches. "What rule? I followed everything—"

"No wandering," he cuts in. "Rule Three. You don't leave your assigned room unless escorted."

"I just stepped out for a second," I say. "I didn't go anywhere."

"A breach is a breach." His jaw tightens. "You triggered an alert."

What alert? I've been on alert my whole life, I can no longer tell the difference.

"Did you ever call Julie? Does she know where I am?"

Alex laughs. He shakes his head slowly. "No. Sorry."

Another dead end.

My stomach twists. "Am I disqualified?"

He studies me, weighing something invisible.

"Not yet. But consequences are mandatory."

"Consequences?" My voice shakes.

"Loss of privileges," he says. "Time allowances. Rest cycles. Meal schedules."

My throat dries. "You mean... more disruption?"

Haven't I already endured enough disruption—the kind that blurs reality and fantasy? This challenge has become brutal. Inhumane.

"There's another rule now," he says, sitting on the bed. "I don't make them. I just deliver them."

"What is it?"

"You're not allowed to sleep during the day."

I laugh weakly. "Why?"

He shrugs. "Not my call."

I shake my head. "I don't understand."

"Read," he says. "Time passes faster that way."

Tears spill down my face.

"You need to understand something," he adds quietly. "This isn't about surviving thirty days. It's about following the rules exactly. If you want the six million—don't slip again."

My knees buckle. "Alex... I'm scared. I'm hearing things—"

"That's part of the adjustment."

"Adjustment?" I whisper.

He nods.

"What is this place?" I ask.

Alex smiles—small, unsettling.

"A hotel that pays well," he says. "But only if you behave."

THIRTY-THREE
RACHEL BROWNING
DAY 5

I haven't slept all night. Not a second.

Which concerns me, given the new rule that has no rhyme or reason: no sleeping during the day.

The only reason I can reckon is to make me break even more. To a point where I stop questioning anything at all.

I consider having another bottle of vodka to knock myself out, but someone has removed all the alcohol from my fridge. Or did I drink them all? Impossible.

There are impulses within me, but drinking isn't one of them.

I sit on the floor, my back against the wall, hugging my legs, rocking back and forth. If I lost count of the days earlier, now I have absolutely no idea how long I've been here.

It feels like years, not days.

I feel the urge to pee. With effort, I stand and plod to the bathroom, holding my stomach. I don't feel well.

I bend over the sink and look up—

A yelp escapes my mouth.

The woman staring back at me looks like she's lived several lifetimes since yesterday. Her skin is sallow, stretched too tightly over sharp cheekbones. Dark shadows pool beneath her eyes, bruised and deep, like sleep has abandoned her entirely. Fine lines carve themselves around her mouth and eyes—lines I don't remember earning, lines that speak of stress, fear, and nights spent staring into darkness.

My hair hangs limp around my face, dull, as if it's given up along with the rest of me. There's gray at my temples. Not just a strand or two—enough that it can't be dismissed as bad lighting or imagination. My lips are pale and cracked, pressed into a thin line that doesn't quite belong to me.

I lean closer, gripping the porcelain sink. My eyes stare back—bloodshot and glassy, too large for my face. They don't look confused.

They look worn.

Like they've seen things I haven't caught up to yet.

I search for something familiar—me—but whatever softness once lived in my features is gone. In its place is a hardness I don't recognize, a brittleness that feels one wrong breath away from shattering.

This isn't what a terrible night does to a person.

This is what time does. Too much of it. All at once.

I swallow. My reflection swallows with me. For the first

time, I don't wonder how long I've been here—I wonder what it's already taken from me.

I turn on the tap and wash my face. The cool water brings brief relief. I feel alive again.

But something inside me is broken.

When I step out of the bathroom, I see it.

A body lying on the floor.

Another scream rips out of me. I clutch the wall behind me, my heart pounding in my head like it's about to explode.

What is a lifeless body doing on the floor of my room? How did it get here?

It's motionless.

I take small steps toward it, my heart hammering, afraid the body might suddenly move—might be alive after all.

As I get closer, I realize it's a woman.

She's wearing a long white dress. Her arms are folded over her chest, her skin pale, her feet pointed stiffly toward the ceiling. Her long hair fans across the floor.

I can't tell if she's breathing.

And then—

"Oh, my God."

I run to her.

It's me.

Rachel.

That's when I sob. I clutch her fragile, unmoving body, my own convulsing with grief.

"Oh, Rachel," I cry. "What happened to you?"

She's dead. Most definitely.

Guilt seeps into my consciousness. Maybe I killed her. If I did, I don't remember how—or why.

The hug suddenly feels hollow.

I lift my head.

She's gone.

Rachel is gone.

"What?" I whimper. "Rachel? Where are you?"

I scan the room frantically, but she's nowhere.

"Rachel!" I scream, tears streaming down my face. "Please—please! Let me take care of you!"

My voice is raw, shredded, but I don't stop. I search everywhere—the bathroom, under the bed, behind the curtains.

Rachel isn't here.

Rage takes over.

I scream at the top of my lungs and collapse onto the floor.

Everything turns dark.

We sit in our rental car—a BMW convertible—heading to downtown LA. I made a reservation at 71Above, the place you need to call many months ahead just for a simple table. It's the place where celebrities wine and dine and dress to the nines.

I didn't need to worry about my reservation. The restaurant owner is one of my many well-off clients, so he made sure I'm always welcome and can get a table at the last minute.

Felecia is sitting in the passenger seat. The air feels warm and crisp as it fills our convertible. Felecia looks worried. She doesn't smile or show that she's happy to be out and about. Her usual M.O., and I'm tired of that, too. Whatever I do to make her happy isn't enough anymore.

The ride is so slow and tedious, I can't wait to arrive at

the restaurant and have a drink. That's another thing about our relationship: I've had my share of alcohol a lot more lately, and I can't handle it.

At the restaurant, we get a good table overlooking the skyline and a beautiful view of the perfect sky, but Felecia still doesn't smile. She fidgets in her seat; something clearly bothers her.

A waiter brings two glasses of water, with lots of ice in them.

Felecia looks into the distance, avoiding my eyes.

I am now annoyed. If there's a single moment we should enjoy our time together, it should be now.

"What is it now?" I speak through clenched teeth.

She glances at me for a second and moves her eyes to the same distant spot.

I lean forward and whisper loudly: "What is it? Talk to me to for fuck's sakes."

I'm using every ounce of myself not to snap and break, but I'm quite close, and Felecia can sense it.

She turns to me and looks me in the eye. "I saw you talking to Mike, your attorney, the other day."

Shock rolls over me, like someone just slapped me on the face for no reason, and I can't quite believe it.

I automatically lean against my chair, gasping for air. Has Felecia been following me? I met Mike in one of the most secretive places, so Felecia or anyone who knows us both wouldn't see me. Why? They would know what the meeting is all about, as Mike is a famous divorce attorney with billboards of his picture hovering all over town.

Mike and I discussed the possibilities of a divorce; not a concrete plan.

I don't like the sound of it. Not a bit. Felecia stalking me, then finding the most awkward time to confront me. In LA. With a whole two days left of our getaway. When a whole slew of things can happen—none of them great, I imagine.

"Wait. What?" I ask, incredulous.

"That's right. I saw you meet Mike." Felecia is unraveling. "Are you planning a divorce?" She averts hers gaze again.

I take a deep sigh and turn to her. "Look. I need to know if you've been taking your meds regularly."

Her nostrils flare at the question. "How dare you ask me this!"

Felecia stands up and runs to the exit. I run after her. "Wait!"

We leave the restaurant without having dinner.

Felecia is having a hard time again. I can just tell. And I don't know how to help her.

WHEN WE GET to the Airbnb, Felecia drops her purse on the kitchen island and runs to the bedroom. Slams the door.

Fuck.

Love can be so confusing. I should have let Felecia go a long time ago, but, let's be honest, I am addicted to her. I can't let her go even if I tried. It's like muscle memory when you try to undo something, but it can't be undone.

Instead of walking to the bedroom to console Felecia, I do what I do best: I grab a beer from the fridge and something to eat too before I pass out.

As I stand looking for what else to grab to eat, I hear footsteps approaching from behind me. The sound of tiptoeing. Is Felecia being sneaky? She has a habit of "surprising me" when I'm in the midst of doing something, as a way to lure me into having sex.

Just as I'm about to close the fridge and turn around, Felecia jumps me from behind. Her arms claw at me like a vulture, so I have no time to respond. We both fall to the floor. I have no room, no time to react.

I am lying on my back on the floor, with Felecia on top of me. "Jesus Christ, what are you doing?" I hiss.

Her face looks like it's overtaken by a million demons, contorted in rage. Her eyes are wild, unfocused, as if she's not seeing me at all but something behind me, something only she can see. Her hands press into my shoulders, hard enough to hurt, pinning me down. I try to twist away, but she's stronger than she looks, fueled by something sharp and frantic.

"Don't move," she hisses, spittle warm against my cheek.

My heart slams against my ribs. I open my mouth to scream and tell her to get the fuck off me, but no sound comes out. All I can think is how quickly this escalated, how a moment ago we were standing upright, and now I'm here, staring up at a face I barely recognize, realizing too late that I misjudged her.

And that whatever this is, it's already out of my control.

And that's when I see it in her hand.

A chef's knife.

She lifts it up, and the edge sparkles against the kitchen lights overhead.

I flinch. What the hell is she doing with the knife? I can assume only one thing: she wants to kill me. What else? That's one thing she got wrong. She doesn't have the physical—or mental—capacity to go through with it. That's the mistake she's making.

"Felecia, please," I plead to no avail.

It's only a matter of time before Felecia presses the knife to my throat and slices it open, leaving me to bleed to death.

There are days she's unhinged, but not like this for Christ's sake. Triggers? Always different, but they all lead back to the same underlying cause. Her childhood memories.

They repeat like a broken record, over and over again. I've never seen her this angry.

"Felecia," I whisper. "Look at me. Put the knife down, please."

She stares at me, and suddenly, her eyes gain more clarity, like someone flipped the switch inside.

The knife drops to the floor, making a loud clink. Felecia starts to sob. And deep inside, I know we're over forever.

Alex hovers above me. I didn't hear him come in.

I'm in bed, wearing a white long dress. I don't remember putting it on.

"Wake up." Alex says in a stern voice. "There's a new rule to follow."

I prop myself with one hand and move the hair from my eyes. "What, what time is it? What day?" I'm feeling like a truck has run over my body.

"Doesn't matter. I'm here to tell you that there's a new rule."

He walks away from the bed, in the door's direction. He turns on his heels and starts laughing maniacally. "Listen, don't kill the messenger, Rachel. I'm just here to tell you what you need to do to win your money."

I have no interest in hearing it. But I have no choice. "Tell me." I whisper.

"You must remain visible to the camera at all times."

It doesn't make sense.

"Wh... why?"

"I've been told you have been acting strangely lately. They want to make sure you're safe. And you don't do anything stupid."

I don't want to admit it, but that checks out. I've been seeing murders, dead bodies, strange objects where they don't belong.

Alex sounds different today. Borderline cocky. Like he's suddenly in charge, and I'm just here to listen to his commands.

His pillbox hat is gone, I notice. He moves his short brown hair to the side, away from his forehead, with his index finger.

"Is that what they told you?"

I see just now he has a duffel bag in his hand. He puts it on my bed and pulls some basic tools and two more cameras.

He glances at me. "Yeah." He turns around and studies the room. "What's the best place to install these?" He's talking to himself more than to me.

He grabs one camera and walks to a far corner, looking at the ceiling like he's taking measures with his eyes. I don't say anything. I watch, resolved that whatever he's doing might be a good thing for me. Yet at the same time, the stakes have been elevated, the truth more grounded: I might be more danger to myself, and that terrifies me.

It takes less than thirty minutes to install two additional cameras. That's another thing that doesn't stand out about him: he looks like he's done this a million times before, which you couldn't tell just by looking at him.

He approaches my bed and cocks his head. "You look scared, Rachel. There's nothing to fear, though. You're safer now." He scans the room and parks his eyes on the books sitting on the table. "Have you started reading yet?"

I shake my head. "N... no."

"You see. You have enough entertainment to last you a month, and you choose to take the hard path."

"I just... I haven't been feeling well. I forgot my anxiety meds at home..." I sniffle and wipe my nose with the back of my hand.

Alex widens his eyes. "Anxiety meds?"

I nod. "Yeah. I really need them."

Alex smiles. "I believe in you. You can control your emotions and behavior without meds, can't you?"

I nod, but I know it's not true. I've got victims' names behind me to prove it: Aaron, Cecilia, Marcia... they all ended up in the ER with an injury because of me. And I was taking my meds. I can only thank God they all survived.

I wonder if Alex somehow knows this. Maybe he really is working on breaking me completely so that I could end up in prison this time, not a mental ward.

"Have you tried meditating?" he says. "Maybe I should get you some books on Buddhism and yoga." He laughs. He walks around the room, placing his hands on the small of his back like he's about to give a TED talk.

"Rachel... have you thought about how evil people get when they're greedy?" he stops and looks at me. I don't even do anything in the way of gestures. "Huh?" he moves again. "What are you gonna do with your six million when you earn it?" he says.

I haven't thought that far. I shrug. "I don't know."

Alex laughs again. "Oh, yes, you do. You're gonna spend it all on yourself, right?"

I gaze down and play with my fingers. "No... I mean..."

He cuts me off. "That's human nature, Rachel. More and more and more. But remember, money won't make you less crazy. In fact, it can make things worse."

I say nothing. I really want Alex to shut the fuck up and leave the room.

Before he leaves, I stop him. "Hey, Alex. I have a question for you."

"What is it?" He says.

"When I first arrived, there were two people who greeted me: Susan and Scott. I think that's their names." We stare at each other. Alex is obviously waiting for the point I am trying to make. "I haven't seen them since."

"Susan and Scott?" Alex repeats.

I nod.

For a moment, he just stares at me. Not confused. Not searching his memory. Calculating.

Then he smiles.

It's small, tight, and completely wrong.

"There's no Susan or Scott," he says.

My stomach drops. "That's not true. They checked me in. They—"

"You're mistaken." His voice is calm now, almost gentle. "We've been over this."

"No, we haven't." My pulse thuds in my ears. "They were here. I spoke to them. Susan had short blonde hair. Scott had—"

Alex steps closer. His shadow swallows mine.

"There has never been a Susan or a Scott," he says, each word sharp. "Not while you've been here."

Cold creeps up my spine. "Then who let me in?"

Alex's eyes flick briefly toward the door.

"You did," he says.

The silence that follows is deafening.

"What?" His response makes zero sense.

Alex reaches for the door handle. "You should get some rest."

The door opens behind him.

Just before he steps out, he pauses.

"And Rachel?" He looks back at me, his expression unreadable. "If you keep inventing people, you're going to scare yourself."

The door closes.

Locks.

I stand there, shaking, replaying Susan's smile. Scott's voice. The way they'd said my name — like they already knew me.

I didn't imagine them.

I know I didn't.

Which means the question isn't where did they go—

It's why does everyone here want me to forget they ever existed?

For the first time since I arrived at the hotel, I am starting to fear for my life.

It's not any kind of fear—it's that raw feeling that clings to you and never lets you go.

What has happened to Alex? And what does it mean there are no Susan and Scott? I saw them with my own eyes —flesh and blood—talking to me, smiling at me. I wasn't dreaming.

This is a pivotal moment in my stay here.

I must find a way to get out of here.

The sound from inside the walls stops me in my tracks. Not a bang. Not a crash. Something softer. Deliberate. A faint scrape, like fabric brushing against plaster, followed by a slow, uneven breath. Then, fingernails scratching the blackboard. I flinch.

I press my palm to the wall, the paint cool beneath my

skin, and freeze. The sound comes again—closer this time, right behind the thin barrier separating us. Someone shifts their weight. Someone exhales. The wall isn't empty. It's occupied. And whatever is on the other side knows I'm here.

The thought disturbs me.

I stand in front of the camera, first watching the red-light blink, then I scream. The scream is so loud, my ears ring from the echo.

I run to the door and wobble the doorknob as hard as I can, but, as usual, nothing happens. The door is locked.

Shit. There's only one way out.

I drag the chairs away from the table and stack them against the door, barricading it. If anyone has already seen me, I don't want them walking in unannounced. At the very least, I'll buy myself some time before they can force it open. There are three chairs in total. I wedge one under the handle, angling it just right, then brace the others against it, my hands shaking as wood scrapes against the floor. It's flimsy. I know that. But it's something—and right now, something feels a hell of a lot better than nothing.

Then I realize: I need one chair.

I move it away from the door and drag it to the window. This fucking window I never figured out how to open, or maybe it was just another trap I have had to contend with.

I stand in front of the window, invisible hands raising my arms, the chair in my hands.

That's when the banging on the door starts. "Rachel, open the door! Rachel, Rachel!"

They must have seen me, now that not one, but three cameras are keeping their eyes on me.

The noise of banging and the knob rattling doesn't stop; it intensifies. The voices continue. Is it Alex's voice? It sounds like there could be more than one. I am not sure anymore.

And quite frankly, I don't fucking care.

With all the strength I can muster, I lift the chair and throw it through the window as hard as I can.

The glass doesn't shatter right away. It cracks—one sharp, spiderweb line slicing across the pane—then explodes outward with a deafening crash. Shards rain down, glittering as they fall, the sound violent and final. Cold air rushes in, slapping my face, carrying the distant roar of traffic and something sweeter: freedom. Behind me, the banging continues. I don't turn around. I step closer to the broken window, glass crunching under my bare feet, my heart slamming so hard it hurts. Below me, the city sprawls impossibly far away.

A voice shouts my name from behind the door, urgent now, panicked. I tune it out, as I feel a lovely breeze of fresh air flickering my hair and my white dress. I climb onto the sill anyway, hands slick with blood, lungs burning. Whatever happens next, I decide, it will be on my terms—not theirs.

I step closer and look down.

It is time for me to free myself.

THIRTY-SEVEN
RACHEL BROWNING

Strong hands grab me from behind. Pull me from the windowsill. At least they are being gentle and not pressing against my flesh.

At the last second, I look at the drop; it's long and deep. If I had jumped, no way I would have survived.

The traffic from the street below hums louder, and it finally brings semblance to my loneliness.

There are three men standing in my room. They broke in after banging, screaming and right on time. Right before I took the leap.

Two men I don't recognize. They are tall, broad-shouldered, and move with a quiet precision. One has close-cropped dark hair; the other has lighter, almost blond hair. Both are wearing plain, fitted shirts and yellow Timberland boots. Even standing still, they seem ready to spring into action.

Is one of them Josh? I don't know. They don't talk much; they just lead me to the bed and slowly place me.

The third is Alex. He's standing in the middle of the room, watching the whole thing unfold, his face blank.

One of the two men walks by him and brushes his shoulder against Alex's. I can't be sure, but he might be mad at him.

The third man kneels next to my bed and checks my vitals: he presses gently on my forehead, checks my pulse, all the works.

I can hear a muffled conversation in the room. "How did you let this happen, for fuck's sakes?" The man sounds angry.

Then silence.

"I... I'm sorry. I stepped out of the room for a while; I didn't see her standing in front of the camera."

"You know Roger will be fucking livid. We almost lost her." The man whispers, but I can hear him. I think I can.

Yet, I don't know why Roger would have anything to do with this. Did he bring me here?

The man continues. "She can't stay in this room. There's a room available on the fifth floor, with no windows."

"Okay," Alex says. "I'll make sure it's ready."

I can hear footsteps rushing out of the room and getting farther away. The traffic below is unstoppable. I look through the broken window and check out the sky. It's blue and vast and whispers secrets.

For the first time in days, I smile.

—————

THAT AFTERNOON, they move me to the fifth floor.

On a stretcher, like I'm an invalid.

The room is smaller. A lot smaller. Whatever pretense of comfort existed upstairs has been stripped away. No soft lighting. No fancy furniture. At first glance, it looks less like a hospital room and more like a ward cell—something meant to contain rather than heal.

The air is stale, unmoving, as if it's been breathed too many times and never replaced. It clings to my skin. I inhale anyway.

There are no tables. No dresser. Nothing anchored the space or made it feel lived in. No cameras either, which surprises me more than it should. Goes against their rules. They were supposed to observe me, but who is going to be watching me now? How will they know I need something? How do I communicate?

There's just a single bed pushed against the wall, its thin mattress sagging slightly in the middle, the sheets tucked too tight, and a side table.

I sit, then lie back.

The metal frame is cold beneath the mattress, seeping through fabric and bone. A shiver runs through me, sharp and involuntary. I pull my arms closer, waiting for the panic to come, for the walls to close in.

Instead, I close my eyes.

I am floating.

The room is chilly.

I feel a gentle rush of air coming from somewhere, but I can't tell from where. I am lying in bed, my hands stiff along my body, and my thoughts are slowly drifting, like I am in some sort of beautiful dream.

I can see my mother running through a field of daisies, with me right behind her, afraid I'll lose her. I am only six years old. Not old enough to gain the speed of an adult, navigating this vast field.

My mother's laughter echoes in the air. It's that beautiful laughter I swear I could hear while I was still growing in her belly. Soft as the murmur of a river. Look at me—lifting my dress so as not to trip, afraid Mom would really speed and take off.

"Mom, wait for me." I yell after her, but she can't hear me.

But Mom disappears.

I stop in the middle of the field and look around for her. I desperately scream for her, "Mom, Mom!" as I spin around.

Where is she? She was there just seconds ago.

Tears roll down my cheeks. I put my head in my hands and sob. My mother isn't supposed to disappear on me like this. Leave me all by myself here...

"Felecia." A whisper. "Felecia!" now a little louder.

I uncover my face from my hands and look in the tree's direction. My mother.

But she's not standing there, looking at me. She's hanging from the tree, her head tilted, her neck looks like it's broken.

My mother is dead.

I SCREAM AND GASP. I sit upright, trying to catch a breath, my lungs burning like I've been underwater too long. My chest heaves, sharp inhales that don't feel like they belong to me. The room snaps back into place in jagged pieces—the bed, the walls, the dim gray light leaking in from somewhere above.

My hands fly to my throat.

It's intact. Whole. No rope. No pressure. Just skin and bone and the frantic thud of my pulse.

I look around frantically, half-expecting to see the tree, the daisies, my mother's dress swaying in the air. But there's only the room. The cold room. The one that never seems to warm no matter how long I lie here.

"Okay," I whisper. "You're fine."

The air returns slowly, reluctantly, as if it's doing me a favor. That gentle rush again—steady, mechanical. Vents. It has to be vents. I turn my head toward the ceiling, but the light is too low to see clearly. Everything here is designed to be just out of focus. Just enough to keep me disoriented.

What day is it? Day 6? Day 7? I say it silently this time, afraid the room might correct me.

My body feels heavier than it should. Not weak exactly—more like weighted, as if gravity has been turned up a notch. I try to swing my legs over the side of the bed, but they respond a second too late. The delay unsettles me.

I press my palm against the mattress, grounding myself. The fabric feels rough, institutional. I hate how it feels against my skin.

The dream clings to me. Not the image of Mom hanging—that part recedes quickly, mercifully—but the field. The way the daisies brushed against my calves. It screams freedom, which has been stripped away from me. For how long, I don't know.

Honestly, I just feel lost. I should have trusted my instincts the second I received the letter. Nobody gives so much money for an experiment.

I stand slowly, testing my balance. The room sways, then steadies. There's a mirror on the far wall—small, narrow, useless. I catch a glimpse of myself as I pass it. Pale. Hollow-eyed. Hair tangled like I've been clawing at it in my sleep.

I look like someone who's been gone for a while.

The door is where it always is. Closed. No handle on my side. I press my ear against it, listening. Nothing. No footsteps. No voices. Just the low hum of whatever system is keeping me breathing.

"How long?" I whisper. Not even a full question. "How long have I been here?"

My stomach twists, empty and sour. Hunger is there, but distant, muted. It feels secondary, like an afterthought. Thirst, too—my tongue dry, my lips cracked—but my body seems more concerned with conserving itself than protesting.

I return to the bed and sit on the edge, wrapping my arms around myself. My fingers dig into my sleeves, as if I can hold myself together by force.

The image of my mother flickers again, uninvited. Not hanging this time. Just her face, younger than I remember it now, eyes bright, hair pulled back loosely. The way she used to say my name, stretching it out like it was something precious.

I lie back down, staring at the ceiling. I count my breaths again. In. Out. Slow. I try to remember the last thing that happened before this—before the room, before the days blurred together.

The Common. Alex. The sound.

My heart rate spikes, but I force it down. Not yet. I'm not ready to open that door again. Some memories need permission, and I don't trust myself to grant it.

Instead, I focus on the cold. The air. The fact that I am awake. Alive. For now.

Time behaves strangely here. It folds in on itself. Childhood bleeds into now. Dreams masquerade as memories, and memories insist they are dreams.

I close my eyes—not to sleep, not really, but to rest them. To float just above consciousness, where things are softer, less defined.

Before I drift off, one last thought settles in, heavy and unavoidable.

Even in my dreams, the ones where I am small and scared and searching, I am always the one left standing in the field.

Waiting.

PART 3

I pace around the small shithole of a room. God, I hate it.

There's nothing redeeming about it. No warmth. No comfort. Nothing suggests anyone ever intended a human being to feel safe here. The walls press in as I move, closer with every step, like they're learning my shape, memorizing it. The air smells faintly of disinfectant and something older beneath it—sweat, fear, resignation. I stop near the corner, hands braced against the wall, and for a moment I consider screaming just to prove I still can. Instead, I swallow it down.

Rage is louder when it's quiet.

I suppose I could read to distract myself from this shit, but I can't concentrate. I can't sit in one place and pretend everything is fine.

Nothing is fine.

Whoever is behind all this needs to be behind bars. Josh? I don't even have his last name. But he could be the one who orchestrated this whole thing, trapped me here like an animal. It has to be some kind of human experiment I never signed up for.

Come to think of it, Josh didn't have me sign any waiver forms, nothing to strip himself of liability.

Why?

He doesn't want any evidence that the experiment ever existed. And if I am right about things like this, I won't be coming out of this alive. Not when they lock you in this small fucking space and hope they will let you walk away unscathed.

Think, think, think.

The breakfast tray is still on the nightstand. I should probably eat before I collapse.

The food is at least decent.

The first few bites give me immediate energy. I'll need it. If I don't escape soon, I will be a victim of this strange scheme forever. I sit on the bed and meditate—think all the good thoughts, force myself is more like it. I picture calm as if it's a place I can walk into, but my mind keeps circling the same sharp edges. The walls hum softly, as if listening. Every sound feels too loud, every second too slow. I tell myself I am still in control, that I can leave whenever I want, but the lie tastes sour in my mouth. Control, I've learned, is just another word they used to keep you still.

I am fully alert. At all times.

The door opens hours later, Alex walking in with a tray of food. Lunchtime.

"How's it going?" he sounds less pleasant this time. Annoyed even. It's like he's just doing this job because he must, not because he enjoys it.

"Good." I smile. "I'm feeling better by the second."

"That's what we want to hear," Alex says, but nothing about it sounds genuine.

"Hey, Alex." I pause. He turns around to look at me. "I think there's a leak in the corner of the room. And I think I smell something sour. It's awful. Do you mind... taking a look?"

He looks incredulous and stares at me for a second too long. "A leak?" he repeats.

I get out of bed. "Yeah, it's over there. I wonder if you could get it fixed, because I'm allergic to mold. It could be that too." I shrug.

He glances at the room's corner, then back at me. "Let me take a look."

I follow every step he takes; I stay close enough. He gets to the far corner of the room, looking at the ceiling, then examining the walls, the floor, the wedge of the walls.

"I don't see anything." He says.

"Oh, no, it's there if you look closer." I tell him.

He squats, and that's when I grab the folding chair. I take two steps and bring the chair down as hard as I can. Alex stumbles, loses his balance, tries to say—"What the fuck..."

But I swing the chair again, and again, and again, and again—the fifth hit does it. He grunts at first and then falls down, his eyes closed.

Alex just lies on the floor unconscious.

I stand there for a second, looking at his twisted body, his eyes closed, his arms helpless.

My chest is heaving. I can barely move, but I have to. I spit at him and say through clenched teeth, "You get what you deserve," then turn around and walk through the door.

For a second, I wonder how long it will take to find him here, but that's not what I should worry about.

The fifth-floor hallway is empty. As I walk to the exit door, I hear voices and TV from behind the doors of the rooms on each side.

The exit door is in the far corner, and I open it casually, pretending I am just any other hotel guest.

When I come to the lobby, there's more life. A lot more people than I'm used to. The main door opens automatically, and I stand there in complete disbelief. No one is here to stop me. No one to chase me. It's just me, looking at my freedom at my fingertips. Just a few steps away. I am about to run away from this place. A sick thought hits me all at once: maybe this is the test. Maybe it always was. They're waiting to see if I'll take it.

I do.

I walk through the door and find myself on the curb, the street in front of me with cars honking and humming. I look at what I am leaving behind one more time: a gigantic sign, The Four Seasons, adorns the triangled building. The luxury. The glitz.

The lie.

I pick one direction and I run.

But it isn't over. I still need a way to get home. I need a phone and someone to transfer me some money.

I run across the Boston Common—it's a perfect day to take a stroll through the park, bring your dog, talk to your neighbor... I am the only one who doesn't belong here. Everyone looks relaxed, like this is the place to soak up all the beauty. Except me.

I look unhinged, frightened, directionless.

Finally, I come to a busy street named Boylston. There's a square in the smack middle of the street, an old church on one side and another enormous building on the other. I take a better look. It's The Boston Library.

Feeling relief, I go inside and ask to use a computer. The lady at the front desk doesn't seem trusting, but she lets me use the computer anyway.

I sit down and start my internet search: Josh Four Seasons.

Maybe the truth hides somewhere closer than it is.

THIRTY-NINE
ROGER
PRESENT DAY

No reason to wait and buy a new house.

I am not staying at my sister's another day, not if I don't want to lose my fucking mind. Don't get me wrong, I love Karen, and she's been nothing but generous letting me stay at her place until I find my bearings, but she also is the most judgmental asshole I know. Too opinionated. Always thinks her advice is the best. She's older than I am, but it doesn't give her the right to treat me like a moron.

I'm sitting at my office, hoping for a call from my real estate agent. He tells me that Las Vegas real estate is not what it used to be: it's a buyer's market now, flooded with desperation disguised as opportunity.

But I am hopeful that something will come up soon.

My phone rings.

Speaking of the devil.

I take my phone out of my pocket, but the phone number

is not my real estate agent's. An unidentified number. I usually don't pick up calls from these numbers, but something whispers in my ear to do it.

"Hello?"

"Hello, is this Roger Mebane?"

"Yes, this is him."

"This is the Boston Police. We're calling to report Rachel Browning missing. Have you heard from her by any chance?"

I look at my phone for a second and put it back on my ear. "Wait, what did you say?"

"Rachel Browning. She's missing, sir."

I pause for a second. Is it possible...? I don't want to take any chances.

"I don't know anyone by that name," I say evenly. "You must have the wrong person."

Silence.

"Sir, you're listed as her proxy in our database. Are you sure you don't know her?"

"I wish I could help you, but I'm positive I don't know a Rachel Browning."

Silence.

"Okay. I understand. Some people don't want to get involved. Have a great day, sir."

He hangs up.

"Rachel Browning?" I repeat, already bored. "Never heard of her."

FORTY

RACHEL

I am sitting at a computer in the cold library, my skin prickling with goosebumps that have nothing to do with the temperature. Libraries are always freezing, but this feels different—like my body never got the memo that I'm no longer trapped.

Every sound feels too loud. The tapping of keys. A chair scraping somewhere behind me. A cough that makes my shoulders tense. I keep my back straight, alert, as if the walls might close in if I relax.

I type Josh Four Seasons into the search box and press ENTER.

A few results pop up.

My pulse spikes.

I click the first one.

A simple webpage loads—barebones, almost cheerful. A

flyer. Josh's face fills the screen, smiling directly at the camera. I recognize him instantly. Those oversized eyes. That calm, practiced expression, like he knows something you don't.

Under his photo, the bold text reads:

Would you like a chance to win $6 million? All you need to do is leave your phone and computer behind and stay at a hotel for thirty days. How hard could it be?

My fingers curl against the desk.

"Fuck you, Josh," I whisper. My throat tightens. "You made it more than hard. You made it nearly impossible."

I click back and open the next result.

A local newspaper article appears, dated June.

Local Entrepreneur Launches Controversial "Thirty-Day Challenge"

Josh Miller, a Las Vegas–based entrepreneur, is drawing attention with a new social experiment offering participants a chance to win $6 million in exchange for a thirty-day stay at an undisclosed hotel—without access to phones, computers, or outside contact.

Miller describes the project as a study in human resilience and modern dependence on technology. "We live in constant noise," he said in a brief statement. "This is about stripping life down to its essentials and seeing what remains."

Critics, however, question the psychological impact of prolonged isolation and the lack of transparency surrounding the conditions of the stay. Miller declined to comment on safety protocols or participant screening, stating only that "everything is voluntary."

The challenge will begin in August this summer. Miller has not disclosed how many participants have completed the program—or how many have quit.

Voluntary.

The word makes my stomach turn.

"Damn you, Josh," I murmur.

At least now I know. At least I'm not imagining things. This wasn't random. This wasn't a misunderstanding. He did this. Whatever that place was—whatever they were doing to me—it was part of his "experiment."

I need to get as far away from Boston as possible. From this place. From him.

But first, I need to call Julie.

I stand and walk to the front desk, my legs stiff, like they don't quite trust the ground yet. The woman behind the desk looks up at me, her eyes drooping with boredom or suspicion —I can't tell which.

"Can I use your phone?" I ask. "Please. I think I might be in danger."

She studies me for a long moment. I'm painfully aware of how I must look—rumpled, pale, frantic. Like someone people cross the street to avoid.

She sighs and gestures toward the landline. "Go ahead."

I pick up the receiver. It feels heavy in my hand. Solid. Real. Something tangible that will help me.

There are only two numbers I know by heart.

I dial Julie's first.

Each ring stretches far and long, my heart climbing higher with each one.

"Come on," I whisper. "Pick up. Please."

The call goes straight to voicemail.

Something inside me caves in. Julie always picks up.

"Fuck," I mutter, lowering the receiver slightly. Leaving a message feels pointless. How do you explain this in thirty seconds without sounding insane?

My gaze flicks to the desk lady. She's pretending not to watch me, but I can feel her attention — sharp and curious. Like she's waiting for me to do something wrong.

I need to move. Now.

There's only one other person I can call. Because Julie's and Roger's phone numbers are all I remember.

The thought alone makes my chest tighten. Roger is the last voice I want to hear. The last person I want to need. But survival has a way of stripping you of pride.

I lift the receiver again and dial his number.

My fingers shake, but muscle memory carries me through.

"Please," I whisper under my breath. "Please pick up."

The line clicks.

"Hello?"

Relief and dread crash into each other so hard I almost can't breathe.

Roger answered.

FORTY-ONE
ROGER

The phone rings again.

I'm not invested; curiosity is the only reason I pick it up. The area code is 6 1 7. Boston, maybe? Sounds familiar.

I answer after the second ring. "Hello?"

"Roger."

"This is him."

"It's me. Rachel." The voice is frantic, urgent, almost vibrating with panic.

It sounds familiar, but the name doesn't match. "Felecia?" I blurt, incredulous. "You—this isn't—Rachel?"

"Yes, Felecia," she says, annoyed, nervous, words tripping over each other.

I stand up from my chair, tension rising.

"When did you change your name?" Josh never told me this important piece of information. "And what the hell is going on?"

"You didn't know you could change your name during the divorce process?" she asks.

I did. But never imagined anyone would go this far—first *and* last name. Well, maybe Felecia. I can picture her hunting for a way to run from herself, erase her old identity.

"Listen to me," she says, voice tight. "I need your help. I was staying at a hotel in Boston for the chance to win $6 million—but I think it's something else. Look it up if you want: Josh Miller." Her breathing is erratic. "Please send me some money before they catch me. Anything. Please. Please."

"Okay, just... relax. Okay?" I sigh. "Can you tell me where you are right now?"

She spits out the answer like a bullet. "I'm in the Boston Library. I'm just... tell me what I need to do."

"Okay, listen to me good," I say. "Let me do something and I'll call you right back, okay?"

"Sure. Sure." She sounds so erratic, I want to hang up on her.

I pause, weighing my options. This could be trouble, big trouble—but leaving her to whatever's waiting for her? Not happening.

"Okay. I'll help you," I say, voice tight but steady. "Give me a few minutes to figure this out. Stand by. I'll call back soon."

"Please hurry before this crazy lady kicks me out."

"Listen. I'll call back soon. Just wait a little longer... okay?"

We hang up. I slump back into my chair, heart hammering, adrenaline pulsing in my veins. Oh, Felecia. You've always been trouble. Some things never change.

A manic laugh escapes me. Part disbelief, part relief, part raw, unfiltered fear. My hands shake as I open my phone and check the call history.

The number from earlier blinks at me. I press it, stomach twisting.

"Boston Police Department, how can I help you?"

I give them Rachel Browning's whereabouts. They thank me, and we hang up.

I dial another number. Someone has some explaining to do. I'm beyond furious that it's come to this—Felecia running away instead of completing the challenge like she was supposed to.

The line clicks.

"Hey, buddy." A cheerful voice comes through.

"Josh, what the fuck is going on?" I snap. "I just heard from the Boston Police that Felecia ran away. What the fuck?"

Silence stretches.

"I'm sorry. I was just about to call you and let you know." He clears his throat. "She hit Alex with a chair and left him unconscious in her room."

My eyes widen. "What?"

"Yeah… I—I had no idea she was so feisty."

"Alex must have done something to bring her to that point? What did he do?"

My body stills, tension coiling through every muscle.

Josh is silent for a few seconds. "I thought you wanted her to break down, did I get that wrong?"

Oh my God. I never told Josh I wanted her to break down. I told him I wanted her to take some time and think things over. Her life choices. And yes, I was willing to pay $6 million for the hopeful transformation. I never wanted her to suffer.

"Listen," I say, my voice sharp. "You need to lure her back in and make her complete the challenge. You got that?"

Josh scoffs. "You really think she'll go for it after everything Alex put her through?"

"I don't care!" I yell. "Come up with a believable story. Make Alex the bad guy. Do whatever you have to—just make her do it!"

I hang up, infuriated. As I collapse into my chair, it hits me: I never asked Josh why he failed to tell me that Felecia goes by a different name.

How long do I have to wait for Roger to call me back?

I pace around the library while the front desk lady follows me with her eyes like a hawk.

Maybe I could pick up a book and pretend to read or anything to look more in control or calm. I sit down at the oval table and put my hands on the top. Waiting, waiting.

The front desk lady comes up to me. "Look, I'm going to ask you to leave now."

"What? Why? I'm not doing anything wrong. Am I?"

"I'm sorry. You're not a member. I can't let you stay anymore." She keeps glancing at the door as if she's waiting for someone to walk through.

"You can't make me!" I raise my voice.

She puts her hands on her waist, cocks her head. "Listen, lady. You need to leave now or..."

The front door opens, and two cops walk in. The

woman's eyes bulge when she sees them, then she looks at me, shaking her head.

"You bitch." I say through my teeth.

"Oh, it wasn't me. I swear." She says.

But I'm not listening to her.

I bolt out of the chair and run. I obviously didn't think through it well, because I pick the direction that takes me to the stairway to the second floor. Before I even reach the first step, one of the cops already reached me and grabbed me from the back.

I shriek in pain. "Leave me alone!" I do my best to free myself. But the cop is way stronger than I am.

They sandwich me in between them as they lead me to the outside. My balance is off, though I'm doing my best to walk straight. The cop on my right pulls me up. The front desk lady is standing in the same place, her mouth hanging open, watching us walk by.

I give her the stink eye and spit in her direction. Some people should burn in fucking hell. Hopefully, karma will get her.

They must have found Alex. He's probably regained consciousness and told them what I've done.

I turn to the cop, "If you think you will break me, you're wrong. I have proof. I have solid proof. And Roger's gonna help me."

It's half true about Roger. How's he going to reach me now?

The cop just looks at me and says nothing.

The cop car is parked in front of the library, blocking one lane of traffic. Not ideal in an already congested area in the town. Passersby are standing by the building, watching the whole show.

I look in their direction and scream at the top of my lungs. "You want popcorn, you fucking pricks!"

"That's enough." The cop says and puts me in the back of the car.

They sit in the front and take off. No sirens, just a normal ride, like they're taking me to a prom.

The city blurs on my side. Brick buildings press close to the street, then pull away. Storefronts with handwritten signs. A Dunkin' on the corner. Brownstones stacked shoulder to shoulder, their stoops worn smooth by decades of feet. Construction cones everywhere, orange and unforgiving.

We pass the Common—bare trees, iron fencing, joggers pretending not to look at the car. Traffic crawls, then loosens. Green lights come too easily. Everything feels ordinary, and that's what unsettles me most. Boston goes on doing what it's always done: buses hissing at stops, pedestrians glued to their phones, the Charles flashing gray between buildings like it doesn't care where I'm being taken.

I want to ask, but I doubt they'll tell me.

I seem to be lost in time and space. It's the worst feeling.

When you can't even tell where you have just been and where you are heading next.

I lean forward, talking to them through the partition while their radio is crackling. "Excuse me, can you tell me what day it is?"

They glance at each other, then one cop looks at me over his shoulder. "It's almost the end of August."

I flinch. It can't be. I was at the hotel for only a few days. I was. At least that's what I am trying to tell myself. And if the cop is telling me the truth, then Alex was right. I was on Day 25. Except I can't remember most of the days I spent at the hotel. Are the cops in it too?

Fuck!

Where are they taking me?

Soon enough, I find out it's not a police station.

They park in front of the familiar building, The Four Seasons, by the Boston Common.

"What... what are we doing here?" I ask, incredulous. They are all conspiring against me.

The cops get out of the car, and one opens the back door for me. "Let's go."

"What are we doing here?" I ask again, but he remains silent.

He takes me under the arm and pulls me toward the hotel door. There, I see a familiar face. He smiles at me and says, "Rachel, welcome back! I'm so happy to meet you in person."

The man standing by the door is Josh.

I've seen him on the screen only twice, but his face is undeniable.

"Rachel, so happy to meet you in person."

He extends his arm to shake my hand. It doesn't make me warm or welcomed; it only raises suspicion about why he's here. But I shake his hand regardless.

The cop lets me go. "Do you need anything else?" he asks Josh.

Josh gives him a quick hand wave. "No, thank you. We're good now."

The cops leave.

"Come here." Josh signals me to get closer. "Let's go to my office and have a chat, shall we?"

"Your office? Do you work for the hotel?"

"Well. Kind of," he says. "I'm actually one of the owners." He smiles. "Please follow me."

He turns around and walks through the lobby, expecting me to be right behind. I do as he asks. I have so many questions. Like, what am I doing here again? Why am I not in handcuffs instead? And what has happened to Alex? Maybe Josh has all the answers. Most likely, he does.

We arrive in his office, nearly the size of the Presidential Suite on the twenty-first floor, just with more fancy electronic devices and lots more wall artwork. A small statue in the corner. I can see now how people like Josh can afford these "challenges" and give away money like it's candy. And he probably doesn't even care about the consequences.

He goes to the bar in the corner, opening a whiskey bottle. "Would you like something to drink?" he says.

"No," I say. "I don't drink."

He pours himself a glass, then walks back to the leather couch and plops himself down. "That's quite admirable. I don't meet many people who don't drink alcohol these days."

I shrug. "I probably would if it didn't hurt my stomach."

Josh smiles. Takes a sip. "Please have a seat."

I look at the single chair opposite the couch and sit down. "I'm sitting. Why am I here?"

Josh's face turns serious. He puts his whiskey glass on the table and leans against the couch.

"Look. Things went horribly while you were here. And

here's the thing. Alex, the guy who was taking care of you? He was an impostor."

I widen my eyes. "I don't understand."

"I don't expect you to. You see, he somehow found out you were the winner of this challenge... went ahead and booked the Presidential Suite on the top floor... and simply pretended that he was one of our employees."

He spreads his arms and puts them on the couch headrest.

"He hired his own people to bring you to the hotel. He removed the clock and TV from the room and installed a surveillance camera. He was hoping that by the end of the challenge, he'd simply take all your money. And the worst part was I had assumed everything was going well. And... that's on me. I am terribly, terribly sorry."

The apology is a good start. Josh tilts his head in remorse. That makes me feel good somehow.

I recount everything that happened while I was here, and the pieces fall into place. Alex refusing to bring a clock. No music. The window. The rules changing without warning. The way he took me to the lobby by the stairs instead of the elevator. Not letting me leave when I asked on so many occasions...

Too many small things. Too deliberate to be random.

And now, finally, it makes sense. This was all on him, pretending he was just the delivery boy.

I am not fully surprised, but a sense of dread still washes over me. To think I was in the hands of an impostor...

"So, the only redeeming thing about him is that he enjoys reading indie authors?"

Josh scrunches his forehead. "What?"

"Never mind." I wave my hand. "Where is he now?"

"Well, you don't need to worry about him anytime soon. He's in custody. The cops will question him, and we're going to discover who is all behind his dirty scheme."

"I am... I'm speechless." I whisper.

"We'll get to the bottom of it soon," he removes his hands from the couch and puts them on the lap. "And that's why we're here now. I'm going to make it up to you."

Butterflies tingle in my belly. I've had enough trauma already. Is there more?

"What do you mean?"

"I still want you to win the money." He pauses. "Just think what you can do with millions after only thirty days."

"You gotta be kidding me!" I squeal. "You want me to do it all over again? No fucking way I'm doing it again." I stand up and run for the door.

"I'll offer an extra million. And you can have whatever you want during your stay except your phone and computer. It will be different this time. What do you say?"

I stop at the door and turn around. "You must be fucking kidding me? After all I've gone through, you think I can trust you?"

Josh cocks his head and puts his lips in a thin line. "Trust me?" Josh meets my gaze. "I get it perfectly. That's why you're the only one I'm asking."

My stomach twists. I hate that part of me—the quiet, traitorous part—that leans in at those words.

I take a step back into the room, then another, until I'm standing beside the couch.

"If I do this," I say slowly, "and something goes wrong—anything—I walk. Immediately."

"Agreed."

"And you don't come near me again."

A pause. Then: "Agreed."

I close my eyes. Just for a second. The silence presses in, familiar and heavy. When I open them, my mind is already made up.

"I'm not saying yes," I tell him.

Josh smiles faintly. "You don't have to decide immediately. Not yet."

But as I stand there, I know the truth. I already have.

"Before we go to my room, can I ask a favor?"

"What is it?"

"Can I make a phone call?"

Josh looks relieved. "Oh, of course. There's a phone on my desk, feel free to use it."

"Thanks."

I walk to his desk and pick up the telephone receiver. I dial Roger's phone number, the one I've dialed so many times. He needs to know everything is fine; I am fine, and that maybe we can talk when I come home.

The phone rings. One, two, three times... Roger isn't picking up. Goes straight to his voicemail. Hmm. Isn't he waiting for my call? Doesn't he know that I need his help? I suspect he'd be sitting by the phone waiting to hear from me.

I hang up the phone and dial again. Josh is circling the room, occasionally glancing in my direction. Smiles.

The phone rings. And rings. And rings—then clicks over to voicemail. Roger isn't answering. A strange weight settles in the pit of my stomach.

He never forgave me for my transgressions. And now... I've lost him forever.

The room is exquisite.

On the twentieth floor, but better than the Presidential Suite by tenfold. Josh is behind me, telling me to go inside.

"Welcome," he says, smiling at me.

I notice a clock on the wall next to the most stunning art pieces hung side by side—originals, not prints—their rich textures catching the light from recessed gold-trimmed fixtures. A large TV dominates the corner, mounted seamlessly into a paneled wall of dark walnut, so sleek it almost disappears when it's turned off. Beneath it, a low marble console holds discreet speakers and a row of neatly arranged remotes, everything precise, intentional.

The room itself feels more like a private gallery than a hotel suite. Plush cream carpeting muffles every step, while a sweeping sectional sofa in soft charcoal velvet curves around a glass coffee table etched with subtle geometric patterns. Floor-to-ceiling windows stretch across one wall, framed by heavy silk drapes the color of champagne, filtering the city lights into a warm, ambient glow.

This is different. Doesn't feel like the last experience.

Crystal accents catch my eye everywhere I look—a sculptural chandelier overhead, a polished decanter set on a mirrored sideboard, brushed brass details along the doors and shelving. The air smells faintly of cedar and something floral, expensive and calming. Nothing here is merely decorative; every object seems chosen to remind you that comfort, beauty, and control come at a price—and that whoever stays in this room is meant to forget the world outside entirely.

"You think you can spend thirty days here on your own?" Josh says.

"Most definitely."

"And look." Josh faces me, his hands up in the air like he's giving an important speech. "If you need anything, absolutely anything, there's an intercom on the wall. You can call the staff anytime. Okay?"

I smile. "Okay." No more cameras and stupid rules of standing and waving in front of them.

Before he leaves, he reiterates that for this to work, I can't contact anyone on the outside—but everything else is up for negotiation.

Josh leaves, the thud of the door echoing in the room.

I stroll to the bathroom, and I'm completely taken by the sight. The shower, the hot tub with multiple jets, and the marble countertops gleam under the soft recessed lighting, making the entire space feel like a private spa I never imagined I'd step into.

"I could get used to this." I laugh.

I go back to the room and see a note on the dresser. The flashback of finding notes in the room with my handwriting makes me jump, akin to being choked in the middle of a nightmare.

But still, I go ahead and read:

Welcome to Day 1! There are only 29 days to go until you get rich! Kick back and relax. We will take care of you. If you need anything, just call the intercom on the wall.

Since this is a luxury hotel where we prefer peace and respect among our employees and guests alike, the only rule we have is: DO NOT DISTURB.

I lower the paper slowly, my fingers smoothing the crease as if the words might change if I touch them long enough. *Do not disturb.* It sounds harmless. Courteous, even. A rule meant to protect peace. I glance around the room—the velvet sofa, the muted lights, the city glowing safely behind thick glass—and feel the familiar pull settle in my chest. The promise of comfort. The relief of not having to decide anything anymore.

I sit. Seven million dollars in thirty days.

This time, Josh and I signed a proper contract. With all the terms and conditions to protect me. It gives me peace of mind.

This time, I don't wonder how I'll get out.

I believe in second chances. I really do.

Felecia—and now Rachel—and I; we weren't meant to be together. I was a fool thinking I could handle her ways, but it couldn't be farther from the truth. Trauma is a heavy burden, and for Felecia, it shapes everything she does. I hate to be that guy, but love alone isn't enough. Call me an asshole—I don't care.

But if it makes you feel better, I still love Felecia, even if it's a different kind of love.

The hard truth no one says out loud: a relationship requires more than love. Patience. Understanding. Acceptance. Both people working on their own issues until they meet in the middle, until they find that last piece of the puzzle. I had that with Felecia. But to build a family? I didn't see us growing old together. And the knife attack in LA—that was the last straw. You can lie to yourself and say it was just a moment of heat, but over time, things spiral. You end up right back at square one.

According to her therapist, ever since she witnessed her father kill her mother, she's seen visions of people being murdered. Not imagined—fixed, like it's the only thing settled in her consciousness. Even the meds couldn't help. The luxury. The good life. Me. I tried, but trying only goes so far.

Yesterday, I signed the papers for a new home. Five bedrooms on two acres. I cashed out my stocks, leaving a comfortable cushion. Thank goodness. The business is stable, and William has kept us out of bankruptcy. A trustworthy partner—one I'll never tire of listening to.

I'm driving to my sister's when the phone rings. Hands-free, I answer. "Hey, buddy. How's it going?"

"Good. You? How's Vegas treating you?" Josh says. My college friend and long-time business associate. His multi-million-dollar hotel ventures always need an interior designer, and we've done plenty of deals together.

Including this "experiment." How did I know she would take the bait and go for it?

I know her well enough to understand that material possessions always seem to heal her—even if it's all made up in her head.

"Hot as hell," I chuckle.

"Listen, it's day thirty," he says, clearing his throat.

"And?" I ask. "How did she do?"

I don't even want to know what Josh told her about Alex —what made her reconsider the challenge.

Josh scoffs. "Better than the first time. I'd say she passed the test."

I'm silent for a second.

"Is she..." I choke, pressing a hand to my mouth to steady myself. "Does she seem content?"

"Oh my goodness. Totally. We took care of her this time. How do you want to proceed?" Josh asks.

I can't back out now. It's all my idea. "I'll wire you the money tonight. And please—no one can find out I'm behind this."

"Of course," he reassures me.

I trust Josh with my life.

"By the way," I say. "How's Alex doing?"

"Oh," Josh chuckles. "He's almost fully recovered. Had a bad concussion but he'll be fine."

I should have seen it coming, Felecia hurting someone in the process, but I had blind faith that she would behave.

"Jesus." I scoff. "Next time, get some meaty guy."

Josh chuckles, "There won't be a next time."

I laugh. "Good point."

I finally arrive at my new home and turn into the empty, quiet driveway. The previous owners are gone. Soon, all of this will be mine—a fresh start. A new life. Maybe a new wife. Maybe kids.

Felecia wasn't it. And that makes me profoundly sad.

Part of me still cares, even if it can't be us. This is why I wanted her to do the experiment: to show her that money isn't everything, that your mind and health matter more. I hope thirty days gave her enough time to ponder, to reflect, and to make the right choices in life. When she walks away from the hotel today, I hope she has learned her lesson.

I know I've learned mine.

EPILOGUE
RACHEL — ONE MONTH LATER

The first thing I learned after leaving the hotel was how loud the world is.

Not the traffic, or the people, or the constant hum of the city—but the choices. The freedom.

Every street I cross. Every door I open. Every text I answer. Every time I decide to stay or leave.

It's noisy like that. It doesn't announce itself until it's taken away.

I live in a small apartment now. I rent it.

It's big enough for me. One bedroom. One bathroom. Most importantly, there are no cameras. No concierge. I checked twice before I signed the lease. The landlord—and older guy named John—thought I was paranoid when I asked about hidden wiring and access points. I didn't explain.

I must look like someone who could afford more. Expensive clothes. Groomed from head to toe. I promised myself to look presentable: physically, mentally, emotionally. It all ties together; it all matters.

John could tell, and nosy that he is, asked why I didn't buy a house instead.

"Buying is a better investment," he said. "It's basically like paying yourself."

I smiled and shrugged.

None of his business.

I don't want roots. I want movement. I plan to travel—sail through the Norwegian fjords, zip line between the trees in Costa Rica, stand beneath the Eiffel Tower and look out over a city that doesn't know me.

I want to enjoy my singlehood and wait to meet a soulmate, if such a thing still exists in this messed up world. Roger wasn't the person for me. When we married, he vowed to be there for me for the good and the bad, and once the bad showed up, he was ready to run.

His vows are just empty words, and I've learned that self-love matters more than anything.

He couldn't wait to divorce me and never see me again.

I heard through the grapevine recently that Josh and Roger teamed up for the experiment. The advertisement and the article about it are real, but I was the only one to receive a physical invitation to submit my application. It was their way of ensuring I would proceed. They'd thought it through from every angle—and made sure there was no room for refusal.

The money came from Roger's account rather than Josh's. I don't know if it's true, but it wouldn't surprise me. He could've just given me the money after the divorce, right? But Roger has always been so self-righteous, looking to prove his point, teach a lesson. I suppose it worked. I had enough time to realize what I want in life.

Mainly peace of mind.

The experiment taught me that. That—and therapy. Lots of therapy.

The windows face east. In the mornings, sunlight spills across the hardwood floors and wakes me before my alarm. I like that. I like being woken by something natural.

My phone sits on the kitchen counter, screen dark. I still flinch sometimes when it lights up, my body reacting before my mind catches up. Trauma doesn't care that it's over. It lingers.

But it no longer owns me.

People think trauma breaks you, that once you're shattered, the pieces can never be put back together. Like when your favorite cup breaks and you glue it back together—it holds, but it never looks the same. Smooth.

I choose to spin it differently.

Sure, I'm a trauma victim, but I'm also a survivor. And that matters more.

Roger? He'll never fully understand that.

I pick up the phone and scroll through the notifications. A missed call. Two unread messages. They're from Julie. I smile, realizing I'll call her back when I'm ready—on my own time.

There's also an email from my therapist, reminding me of today's appointment.

I answer none of them. Freedom is enough.

I make coffee instead. I take my time—measuring, pouring, waiting. No one is watching the clock. No one is taking notes. No one is deciding whether I'm improving fast enough.

It's only nine in the morning, but I turn on the Bluetooth speaker and blast music, my favorite song by Elton John, *I'm still standing*.

I dance and dance until sweat breaks out. I sing at the top of my lungs and I feel damn good.

Later, as I leave for my appointment, I pause in the lobby. A security camera—the only camera I've accepted—is mounted above the front door. For a split second, the old instinct surfaces, urging me to lower my gaze, to move carefully, to behave.

I don't.

Outside, the city moves around me, indifferent and alive. Cars honk. Someone laughs too loudly across the street. A dog pulls at its leash, desperate to go nowhere in particular.

I step into the noise. I close my eyes and take a deep breath.

I choose the direction.

And for the first time in a long while, the world doesn't feel like a test.

It feels like mine.

ABOUT THE AUTHOR

Nadija Mujagic is the author of several psychological thrillers. She lives in Massachusetts with her husband, son, and their beloved standard poodle, Koko. When she's not writing, she enjoys playing sports and jamming on her electric bass guitar.

CHECK OUT OTHER BOOKS BY THE
AUTHOR — SCAN BELOW

CONNECT WITH THE AUTHOR ON
INSTAGRAM - SCAN BELOW

CONNECT WITH THE AUTHOR ON
FACEBOOK - SCAN BELOW